To my
Friend.
I hope you enjoy
this as much
as I Did.

Willie

RECOVERING FROM

DYSFUNCTION

You are not alone!

Paul

Zeph 3:17

RECOVERING FROM DYSFUNCTION

YOU ARE NOT ALONE!

Paul Bishop

Zion Press

Zion Press
1601 Mt. Rushmore Rd, STE 3288
Rapid City, SD 57702

Ordering Information:
Quantity sales. Special discounts are available on quantity purchases by corporations, associations, and others. For details, contact the "Special Sales Department" at the address above.

Recovering from Dysfunction/Bishop —1st ed.

ISBN 978-1-63357-324-6

Library of Congress Control Number: 2020936310

First edition: 10 9 8 7 6 5 4 3 2 1

This is a work of historical fiction. All incidents and dialogue, and all characters with the exception of some well-known historical figures, are products of the author's imagination and are not to be construed as real.

Praise for
Recovering from Dysfunction

"Not only will you better understand some of the important (and dysfunctional) people that God has used to accomplish His purposes, but you will also see your very own self in these stories, or someone you know. So—get ready to understand yourself and others in a new way! Get ready to hear the Lord speak and change you from the inside out. These inspired stories are the very ancient paths that will lead us all home. Thank you, Paul Bishop, for nudging us heavenward where our true help and healing comes from!"

> **—John Fletcher**, senior vice president of Global Missions,
> Pioneers

"I find myself identifying with the Bible characters and their life story. 'I see that, I feel like that. Wow! God used people with flaws and they had to learn to trust and depend on him. Maybe God could use me?' The questions at the end of each chapter make for great group discussions and the practical principles provide a path to follow."

> **—Ralph Schneck**, lead pastor, First Baptist Church
> (Lexington, SC)

"Unique perspective, thought-provoking questions, easy to read . . . addiction counselors will find this book to be a useful tool for Christian clients. The humanity of biblical characters is highlighted in a narrative style, enabling readers to quickly envision the overlap and application in their own lives."

> **—Leah Herod**, PhD, licensed clinical psychologist

"This short book has the potential to be much more than a quick read about biblical characters. In all kinds of Bible studies, men's and women's groups, this book could be the practical means by which people begin to let go of some of their 'baggage' and actually move on toward godliness and peace."

—**Stephen H. Farra,** PhD, LP, senior psychology professor, Columbia International University

"While *Recovering from Dysfunction* reminds me I am NOT alone with my hurts and hang-ups, the book's greatest success is in reminding me that the solution is not as far away as I once thought."

—**Jim Sonefeld**, musician, Hootie and the Blowfish

"In *Recovering from Dysfunction*, the reader is invited to enter into the everyday lives of these characters and to listen to them tell their stories. Because of his extensive experience in working with individuals in recovery, Paul shows us how to empathize with these real people who faced many of the same issues we face today. By combining his rich clinical experience with some wonderfully creative writing, Paul is able to capture the life lessons these stories were intended to provide."

—**Larry R. Wagner**, PhD, professor and psychologist, Columbia International University

"Very thought-provoking and knowledgeable . . . I love this book."

—**Ken Jumper**, pastor, The Harvest (Lexington, SC)

Thanks, Paul, for bringing to life the characters of the Bible. When you hear about people of the Bible you think they were super heroes or that they did not experience life as we do today. Paul has brought them to life and has given hope to people today in how God has worked throughout history. This is truly a message of hope in a time of despair.

—**Bobby Sledge**, Celebrate Recovery Leader

This book is like absolutely no other and gives an extraordinary look into the lives of some Bible characters who struggled with many of the exact same hurts, habits and hang-ups that each of us still struggle with today. I can assure anyone who reads this book that you will not remain untouched and unchanged by hearing the struggles and victories of each individual as they journey into awareness and recovery. You will find the encouragement and support that you will need as you continue on your own journey.

—**Stacy Mink**, Celebrate Recovery Leader
Nonprofit Community Advocate

Contents

Acknowledgments

So many I couldn't do without:

Without Jesus Christ as my Higher Power, I would still be a raging codependent going through life without boundaries and with constant anxiety over whether the world accepts me.

Without the support of my wonderful wife, Susan, I would not have known the personal and freeing nature of God's love and grace. Her support for this project, and grace with the time that was involved, was invaluable.

Without the foresight of our lead pastor, Ralph Schneck, who pointed me in the direction of a Christ-centered twelve-step program for our church, I would not have known about Celebrate Recovery.

Without the vision of John Baker and Celebrate Recovery, I would not have been exposed to such a healthy and freeing set of principles and steps toward recovery and healing.

Without the many individuals who have had the courage to step up and share their own stories in Celebrate Recovery at First Baptist Church of Lexington, I would not have been inspired to explore the stories of the individuals in the pages of this book.

Without the direction and skills of Don Hampton, Stacy Mink, and the editors at CrossLink, who took time to read every chapter, making valuable editing suggestions, you may have had a harder time reading what you hold in your hands!

I want to thank each of you, and countless other friends, family members, and mentors who have been part of my story and have allowed me to be part of yours.

May the Lord bless and direct your own story of recovery, and may this book help along that journey.

Paul Bishop

Introduction

G od did not create our dysfunction, and he does not condone our mistakes. Our Father in heaven is the perfect member in this huge family—lovingly waiting, without a codependent need to rescue, but with a heart full of compassion to redeem. Our choices are not his fault. Our consequences are not his responsibility. Our healing is the desire of his heart, however; and our redemption is his purpose. That is the truth we must hold onto on our journey to become the people we were created to be.

The reality is that God has placed before us models from which we can learn. People in the Bible really were no different than people today. They struggled with all the same temptations and failures we know—they ticked each other off and fought addictions, isolation, depression, and anxiety. They hurt each other, helped each other, and sometimes even betrayed each other. They laughed together, cried together, and sometimes fought together. In other words, they were human—just as we are human. Their stories are our stories, and from those stories we can learn valuable lessons, be challenged, and draw hope.

The idea for this book came from my own experience over the past fifteen years as the ministry leader in Celebrate Recovery. Week after week, I have listened to people share how the Lord has redeemed the struggle and recycled the pain in their own lives to bring purpose and healing. As a licensed counselor, I daily hear the pain and brokenness that is universal for all of us—the same themes I find in Scripture. No pain is too great for God to heal. No mistake too severe for him to forgive. No man or woman is too broken, damaged, or far from his reach that God cannot draw that person to himself, and use their woundedness for His glory. Purpose is in every story; and if we will listen hope is for each of us on the road beyond dysfunction.

Although none of the characters in *Recovering from Dysfunction* attended a Celebrate Recovery meeting, I have attempted to imagine how they would have shared their stories if they were to show up at one. At Celebrate Recovery, we seek to maintain a humble awareness of our areas of struggle and yet place our identity in our Higher Power and not our dysfunction. We begin with an introduction that reflects this and close with thanks to those who listened for letting us share. We share in our stories how we got to where we were, how God got our attention, then led us to where we are. We seek to be honest with our past, realistic about our present, and hopeful for our future.

Nobody knows all the details of the stories presented here—how the people felt, why they did what they did, and sometimes even what was said. I've done my best to stay true and accurate to the biblical account while seeking to dramatically envision what might have moved them—the emotions, events, and situations in which they found themselves while on their individual journeys. The goal here is to be true to God's Word and to connect the stories of these people to the deeper aches and experiences within our own stories—to help us be more deeply involved in Scripture while also finding profound healing in the reality that the Lord redeems all if we will but yield to him and allow him to rewrite our story.

I hope God uses each of these stories to offer you hope in your own journey. No matter where you are along the way, your story is not over. Where you have been does not need to determine where you are going! God's love and mercy extends far beyond any dysfunction, any past action, or any deep wound we might bring with us. The wonderful news is that he loves, forgives, and chooses to heal us in spite of our dysfunction because of the patient Father that he is.

Lost Identity; Renewed Hope

(Hagar's Story)

I have a hard time believing that my story is worth telling. I've lived most of my life as a servant for wealthy families. Actually, my identity was wrapped up more in who I worked for than my own value as a person. I am learning, however, that my story is part of God's story, and I hope that you may benefit from hearing what he has done in my life and how my weaknesses have been redeemed through his strength. I am a single, divorced mom, mother of Ishmael. I struggle with identity issues. My name is Hagar.

I grew up in a family of slaves. Our lives and feelings of success depended upon those we worked for, and there was no such thing as a career change. When I became old enough to have my own master, I was lucky enough to work for a couple named Abraham and Sarah. It was a far better environment than the homes where most of my brothers and sisters ended up working.

Abraham and Sarah believed in Jehovah and tried to treat their servants right. My identity became more and more that of Sarah's trusted servant. Working for a wealthy family helped my standing with other servants, and some of them were jealous of my position. I did not initially have too much contact with Abraham, and I answered to Sarah, as her chief assistant. Overall, life was going well and had surpassed the low expectations that I had set for myself.

One day all of this changed. I began to hear Sarah talking about having a baby. This had been a sore spot throughout their marriage, as they had not been able to have children. I had heard her talk about her regrets and disappointments and even feeling like a failure for this. I was often her sounding board. It was not surprising that Sarah wanted a child, but it was extremely surprising that she somehow was thinking this would happen now that she and Abraham were in their nineties. Apparently they had received a message from God regarding this happening, and Sarah was struggling, more than Abraham, to believe this would actually occur.

The most surprising conversation came the day that Sarah let me know that she wanted me to become a second wife to her husband. She informed me that she was not only totally OK with it but that she had convinced Abraham and that I was to marry him immediately. My role was already less of a servant, and oftentimes more of a friend to Sarah, but how would this impact things? Will she really want me as a second wife to her husband? I knew it was a common practice in the area, but it was less common with those following Jehovah, and I was confused and conflicted.

But then again, I was a servant, and I only had to comply. Maybe it would be nice to be with a man and to actually be a wife and not just a servant any longer.

This would not be a typical marriage. While Sarah wanted me to be with her husband, her motivation was that of having a child in the family that would carry their name. As tender and kind as Abraham was, I could not help but question if he really wanted me for who I was or simply for what I could offer. Was I being used? Or was I being loved? Was I now considered an equal? Or was I still simply a servant, offering a service?

My questions haunted me at nights when I lay in bed and wondered how things would play out. I began to resent Sarah and wished I could have Abraham all to myself. I enjoyed my evenings with him and secretly wished I did not have to share him with Sarah. I went back and forth from feeling insecure about my future and how long I would have Abraham's favor to being prideful and to treating Sarah with contempt. I knew this was wrong, but I was powerless over my emotions and of the way I was developing a negative attitude toward Sarah.

Soon it became obvious that she had had enough of my attitude, and Sarah seemed to resent my place in her husband's life as much as I had come to resent her. I had sensed the resentment at times when I was pregnant and had to get off my feet after a long day. She never had children and did not understand what this was like. I became proud and forgot where this blessing had come from. She longed to have a baby of her own. Her jealousy became more and more obvious, and I often saw Abraham caught in the middle.

He would tell her that she could "deal with me" as needed, but then quietly reassured me that he would always provide for and look after me as well as our child who was on the way. Sarah's jealousy caused her to treat me harshly. It seemed she would be glad if I was out of the picture. I no longer felt cared for or looked after by her, and one day I had all that I could take of her catty remarks and sarcastic comments about me being "just a slave." I was afraid to raise my child with Sarah and afraid of my own feelings when around her.

I decided I would have to start over somewhere else. I ran away.

I wandered away and was soon all alone. While contemplating my future and wondering how a pregnant mother would get a new position elsewhere, I saw a being standing in front of me. It was an angel representing the Lord, and he reassured me. Regardless of how this all transpired and despite how I had handled things, God assured me that he was going to redeem my situation. He could use Ishmael and me, and he had other plans for my future and for my descendants. I still had a purpose. I needed to get back to my post and submit to Sarah and keep my attitude in check. In this moment, I came to realize that there is a power greater than myself and that he truly loves me! Maybe he could help me go back and try again. It took everything in me, but I swallowed my pride and went back, asking Sarah for another chance. She gave this to me, but things were never the same, and I felt that she held this over my head for years to come.

My pregnancy progressed, and the day of delivery soon arrived.

It was a proud moment when Ishmael was born and lay upon my chest. Everyone was excited, and I truly felt like we had something that may bring us all together again. My identity was no longer just that of slave but now included that of mother. I had nagging worries about whether Sarah would take over raising this child and whether Abraham would still want me after I had given them what they needed. After all, Sarah was his first love, and I was still a servant. When I had doubts, I would remind myself of God's reassurance, and I tried very hard not to get caught up in the emotional whirlwind of our complicated life. I also began to see, however, why God intended one woman for one man in his original plan for families.

After Ishmael was born, Sarah tried to spend time with him, but as he became hungry, the reality was that only I could breast-feed. I sensed further bitterness from her. She wanted more and more to decide how to deal with Ishmael when he misbehaved, and she wanted Abraham all to herself. Ishmael was a strong-willed child. He loved the outdoors and did not want to play inside or to be told what to do.

We had moments where he lost his temper or bullied the other servant children on the compound. Abraham was always patient and able to give me support and guidance in how to teach him. I actually welcomed these moments with Abraham because they reassured me that I meant more to him than just a servant wife. It kept us connected. I knew Sarah expected Ishmael to take their family name and that I would be required to stay in the background as he got older. But I could put up with this so long as I had a safe place to live, and a family, no matter what my role.

Some days were hard; others were bearable. Just as I began to think we were going to make it, the unbelievable happened. Sarah became pregnant at the age of ninety! Neither she nor Abraham could hide their excitement. I had mixed feelings. On the one hand, I wondered how they would feel about me once they had their own son. Would my role become unnecessary? Would Ishmael still be welcome? I now doubted that Ishmael would be the heir, although this had been promised to me over and over. On the other hand, I did hope that having her own child would help Sarah to let go a bit and let me raise Ismael without her interference. I prayed hard and sought to release my fears and anxieties about the future to God and to focus on one day at a time.

About the time that Isaac was born, Ishmael was getting older, and his wild streak was growing worse. Isaac would run to Sarah crying, accusing Ishmael of making fun of him or picking at him in some way. Sometimes I truly believed that he was making things up for the extra attention that he would receive. As much as I knew Ishmael should not pick on Isaac, I also understood that he carried resentment from the birth of Isaac.

He was no longer the heir, no longer the only son, and no longer the focus of everyone's attention. I tried to help my son and sometimes would overlook what he said or did to Isaac, knowing how he must be feeling underneath his anger. Sarah was much too hard on him, and I tried to counteract this with a softer approach.

When Isaac was ready to be weaned, they planned a large celebration, and all the relatives were invited. This was a big event in our culture and a time to celebrate the fact that a child was no longer dependent upon the mother for milk and was now ready to eat solid food. Ishmael did not have as large a celebration, and I was feeling a bit resentful when Sarah informed me of all that I had to do to prepare this feast and celebration for her son. Yes, I was the servant, but I also was a wife and mother now, yet she seemed to expect me to do all the work.

As everyone focused on the boy, I could see Ishmael becoming angry and cynical. He didn't want to be there, but Abraham told him that he needed to stay. Before long, he began teasing and picking at Isaac when he wobbled or lost his footing. At one point, Ishmael's imitations and making fun of Isaac caused me to chuckle and join in with him. I should not have laughed at him, but I did.

Just then, Sarah looked over in my direction. Her eyes were like darts, staring me down and accusing me of much more than I deserved. Immediately I saw Sarah talking to Abraham. She was angry, and she'd had enough. I overheard her telling Abraham that he had to choose and that one of us had to go. Now I was afraid. What if he agreed to send us away?

I lay in bed that night hopeful that this was all a misunderstanding and that Sarah had spoken impulsively. I prayed that by morning, she would change her mind. Surely the years that she had helped care for Ishmael would cause her to rethink such a decision. After all, she was the first one to hold him the day he was born. Perhaps Abraham would tell her that he could not send us away.

Morning came, however, with no such change of mind, and I was awakened from my restless sleep with Abraham nudging me and handing me a water bottle and some food for our journey and sending us on the way. He had tears in his eyes as he painfully embraced each of us and told Ishmael that he would always love him. He kept his words short, as Sarah was glaring from the other room, making sure that Abraham followed through on her demands.

Sarah had little to say. She tightly held Isaac, as if to protect him from us, as we walked out the door.

It felt like a bad dream, and I could not believe that this was really happening. This home was all I had known. Sarah had been good to me in the past. How had it come to this? Abraham was the only man I had been with or been married to. Despite the circumstances of being a "servant wife" and having to know my place, he genuinely seemed to care about my well-being, and he often had comforted me and reassured me when I was struggling with my position. He was the one who told me that he would always provide for me and for our son. He said our son, Ishmael, would be the heir of God's promises.

Now, I wandered in a daze, feeling betrayed, abandoned, and deceived. I questioned if any of it had been true. Was I ever more than hired help to this man and woman? I recalled faces of the other servants, their children laughing on the estate, and the joyful singing and dancing when our work was done. I even began to long for the camels, the sheep, the goats, and the chickens roaming the property. So much I had taken for granted. Now I had no idea where or when I would have my next meal.

It would have been one thing starting over on my own. But now I had a son to think about and another mouth to feed. Abraham meant well, but the meager supplies he loaded us down with could only go so far. The water was running out and the landscape was looking dusty and dry. I began to imagine my son's death in the wilderness, unable to find water or food. What a horrible death this would be, alone, body dying of starvation and overcome by thirst.

The grief I felt over a lost identity and the loss of everything I had known was soon diminished in comparison to the anticipation of losing my son. Where was this God I had met years earlier? What had become of his plans for my son's future now? Perhaps God was no more real than the elusive family that I thought I had gained with Abraham and Sarah.

As I wandered farther and farther away, the desert became drier, and the landscape grew browner. I was angry that Sarah was so overly sensitive. I was hurt that Abraham was so nonchalant and passive. I was upset at Ishmael for getting us kicked out of there. I was angry at myself for being too soft on him, for laughing at his antics, and for not being stronger. I was confused by a God who I believed in for all these years. I began a down-ward spiral of negative and catastrophic thinking. We had now run out of water, and here we were stuck in the middle of the desert.

Without water, Ishmael would not survive. Without Ishmael, I had nothing left to live for. I was losing all hope.

If only I had never met Abraham and Sarah. If only I had not agreed to marry Abraham. If only I had kept my mouth shut around her and not antagonized her. If only Ishmael had not started teasing Isaac. If only I had been a better parent, a better servant, a better wife, a better person. If only we had gone the other direction when we left home. Once you allow your mind to go down that track, the "if onlys" keep coming. I was on a down-ward spiral and was soon wondering how long until we would both be dead. If Ishmael died first, I knew that I would take my own life. I could not stand to go on without the only family member I had left!

I did not want to lose control in front of my son. I found a shaded bush where he could be comfortable and left him there as I walked away to where he would not see me crying. He was soft-ly weeping and looked so vulnerable. I should have stayed and held him, but I was not thinking clearly, and I left him there. As I stood alone about one hundred yards away from him, the flood-gates opened, and all my fears and sadness overflowed through each teardrop that poured down my face. My body crumbled un-der the emotional weight, and I sat there crying, feeling com-pletely helpless and all alone.

Suddenly out of nowhere, a familiar voice called to me and asked me what was wrong. I was embarrassed to have left my son alone and was afraid of being looked down upon, but the voice did not condemn me. It told me not to be afraid. This was a gentle voice, a reassuring voice. I recognized this as the voice of that being who had met me when I ran away before, the one who had promised me he would look after my son. He went on to say that he had heard my son's cries, not just mine. He still had plans for my son that included making a great nation from him. Then as my heart softened and I began to believe and hope again, I saw it! Right off to the side, there was a well of water. I had not seen it before. I did not even look before. I did not have any reason to hope or believe there were any resources around me until now!

It was a miracle—not that the water had suddenly appeared, but that the eyes of a woman who was bitter, hopeless, and ready to die had been opened. I quickly filled a bottle with water and ran over to my son. His eyes, red and swollen from crying, slowly opened. He drank and drank, then we went and got some more water, laughing and thanking God for his provision. This was not the end of my story or Ishmael's but the beginning of something new. He grew to become a successful hunter, married a lovely young lady, and we were given the blessings that God had promised.

No, it did not happen the way I had expected, nor in the place I had expected. But God had not forgotten me, and he had known all along how he was going to provide for us! Even when you feel that you have lost it all or that the future is hopeless, don't give up! I could not see the future, and I temporarily failed to trust the one who does.

If you have felt abandoned, forgotten, neglected, or alone, I know how that feels. Don't trust your feelings, but choose to trust the God who still has a plan for you. I lived most of my life with the identity of being a servant. Today, I am still a servant, not of another human being, but of the one who created me. I am choosing to trust him, who holds the future, even when I cannot see the future that he holds for me.

Thank you for letting me share.

Questions for Reflection:

1. Do you relate to Hagar and her struggles with her identity? If so, in what ways?
2. What were the sources of conflict between Hagar and Sarah?
3. When have you felt that the future was hopeless and struggled to go on? How did you get past this?
4. Do you ever struggle with the "if onlys"? What does that look like for you?
5. The Lord showed Hagar a spring that she had failed to see. In what ways have you had resources around you that you had failed to see? What were they?
6. What resources has God provided for you today?
7. If you are a parent, how hard is it for you to trust God with your children?

Principles for Recovery

1. Place your identity in the one who never leaves you, not those who do.
2. Sometimes your greatest resource is already there, but you haven't seen it yet.
3. While you focus on what could have been, you lose sight of what might still be.
4. Waiting for God's plan prevents the painful mistakes that often come from proceeding with ours.

Resentment and Regrets; Repentance and Reconciliation

(Judah's Story)

I have struggled all my life with guilt from betraying a brother who I deeply resented, from lying to others, and from sexual immorality. I also experienced the loss of two sons and a wife. I am a grateful believer who God led to repentance and reconciliation. My name is Judah.

My story began in a fairly dysfunctional home. My father married my mother only after having been deceived by his father-in-law. His first choice and intended bride was not my mother. Stuck with my mom, he then made a new deal with my grandfather that he would work another seven years for her hand in marriage. There was always tension in the home between my mom and Rachel, Dad's other wife. My mom lived with the knowledge that she was not the favorite, but she found comfort in having children. In fact, she was blessed with several children long before Dad's other wife ever became pregnant. I was one of them.

Things became complicated when Dad's other wife asked my dad to take her servant to be a third wife. She did this primarily so she could feel that some of those children also belonged to her. The rest of our childhood was consumed with jealousy and competition, bullying and lying. When all was said and done, Dad had four wives, including Mom, Mom's servant, and Rachel and her servant. While we had some advantages of a large family of siblings, we also had our share of conflicts. I often felt stuck in the middle between my mom and the kids of the other moms and found it difficult to get dad's attention, especially after Joseph came along.

Joseph was the favorite for several reasons. He was the first-born from the favorite wife, Rachel. He was also Mr. Perfect, who could do no wrong. He relished this role. He made sure the rest of us knew that he was having dreams from God and appeared to believe that he was a bit better than the rest of us. Whether that was his intention or not, this was how the rest of us perceived him, with the possible exception of his baby brother, Benjamin. To make matters worse, Dad gave him a spectacular coat—the only one of us to receive such a gift. Every time I saw that color-ful coat, it reminded me of how much Dad loved him. It made me wonder why I never received a coat like that.

The rest of us would be working in the hot fields all day while Joseph had the easy jobs back home or of being the delivery boy and bringing us our lunch. This was so unfair that it began to eat at me every time I saw Joseph approaching, especially when he was parading that coat!

It was one of those days when we were out watching the flocks, getting hungry, thirsty and worn out in the heat, when here he came! Sure enough, he had that coat on! You could not miss it. It was the most colorful item of clothing in the land. It shouted the words, "I am the favorite!" "Dad loves me more!" "I am the chosen one!" My brothers and I started venting, "There he is!" "I wonder what kind of dream he is going to tell us about today?!" "I can't believe he told that one about us all bowing to him the other day!" "I wish that boy would keep his mouth shut!" "Did you hear dad bragging to the neighbors about him last week?" "Things would be so much better at home if Joseph were not here!"

What began as letting off steam just among ourselves soon morphed into a plan of how to get him out of our lives alto-gether. Thinking back, it sounds terrible! Hearing everyone ex-pressing the same feelings and feeding off one another took the conversation to a whole new level! Maybe we would be doing ourselves a favor. Maybe he didn't deserve to live in our family with his arrogant attitude. Maybe if we took him out quickly, it would not hurt too badly. We could just tell Dad that a wild animal got him.

Before we realized what we were doing, we had a plan devised. Thanks to our more responsible older brother, Reuben, we were convinced to hold off on taking his life until later and threw him in a pit. When we heard some slave traders coming through on their way to Egypt, we told ourselves we were doing him a favor by selling him and not killing him. I was actually proud of myself for coming up with the genius idea of letting him live out his life as a slave while we would carry on without him. Amazing how rationalization can work to ease a guilty conscience!

The guilt kicked in pretty quickly, however, when we went back to the house at the end of the day and faced Dad. I don't think I will ever be able to forget the anguish in Dad's face as he looked at the blood-stained coat that we used to sell our story that Joseph had been killed by a wild animal. For months on end, Dad stayed in the house—dejected, hopeless, lethargic, and often sitting alone staring off into the distance. I tried on numerous occasions to comfort him. It was strange knowing that the son he was grieving for was still alive, though living in slavery.

I did everything I could to comfort him, never betraying our story that Joseph was dead. How my heart ached, watching my dad, once a vibrant and confident man, slowly fading away from grief. I saw the impact on Joseph's mom, Rachel, and even my mom, who tried in vain to comfort them both. The voices in my head began to beat me up with thoughts of what we had done, how it had destroyed Dad's life, and fear of what had become of my little brother.

Soon, I could not take living at home any longer. I could not take seeing Dad mourning this way. I learned of a room for rent with a man in a neighboring town. Maybe this was the answer. I did what I could to escape the memories of our failures. I married a local woman, knowing she was not of the same faith but not caring anymore. I doubted that God wanted anything to do with me anyway. She was attractive, and at this point, I needed someone to make me feel better. I liked feeling what I did with her and it helped me forget, and there was a lot to try and forget. I wrapped myself up in my new family life. We had three sons together and poured ourselves into their lives. All seemed to be going well. I helped my oldest son find a wife. I was excited about the prospect of soon being a grandfather!

It was then that my world was once again turned upside down. My oldest son died unexpectedly. I watched my wife and my daughter-in-law go through intense grief and tried to console them, much as I had my father, even as I tried to deal with my own emotions. I told my next son that it was his place, as was our custom, to marry our oldest son's grieving widow, Tamar. This was the plan that allowed us to carry on our family line, and it would give her comfort to have a child. It would give us all comfort. My son was resentful, however, and did not want to have a child with her and failed to do his part. Soon God took his life as well.

I had lost two sons, and now people were saying that it would be my third son's place to marry her. I was afraid, though, after losing two sons who were married to this woman. Maybe the same thing would happen to him? Perhaps I needed to protect him and keep him home with us. There was no way I was ready for another risk. I would tell her that this boy was too young and send her home to her parents, then just find other excuses later to avoid losing another son to this woman.

With no intentions of contacting her, my daughter-in-law soon caught on to this and realized she would not be hearing from me. My wife died, and I soon filled my emptiness the only way I knew how—by running. I ran to other towns, to other women, to prostitutes, and to business deals that could keep me busy. My daughter-in-law began to hear of my reputation and knew that I was not above seeing prostitutes. While I thought nobody knew what I was doing, I was the last to realize that they did, as I had become less discreet in my encounters. One day, Tamar heard that I would be coming that way on a business deal, and unbeknownst to me, she came up with a scheme that would bring me to a new low.

"Wait here a couple hours," I told my friend. "I am going to spend a little time in town." He had learned to look the other way but knew good and well what I was up to. As I headed down the usual road where I knew I could get some action, there was a young, beautiful woman along the road making it very obvious that she was available for the right price. The adrenaline rush began, and I was in pursuit. Though I still felt the pangs of guilt along the way, there was always that short time of pure escape and gratification where I threw caution to the wind and indulged, with no thoughts of the past, the pain, or the regrets. Once I was with this woman, there was something oddly familiar about her. She said little, but when she spoke, I knew I had heard this unique voice somewhere. Yet I had no recollection of seeing her around here or of being with her before. Something was different, and the guilt consumed me once again. I pushed those strange feelings to the side, got dressed, and got out of there as soon as I could.

When she agreed to have sex with me, I had promised to send a goat as payment. In exchange, she had held onto my one-of-a-kind identification seal and my personalized walking stick. Looking back, it was a very foolish agreement. At the time, however, l was only looking for how to get what I wanted at that moment. I failed to "play the tape" to where this could go. I asked my friend to deliver the goat on my behalf in an effort to preserve my own dignity. Regardless of how much I excused my own sinful choices, I knew they were wrong, and I did all I could to keep them a secret.

My secrets were piling up, and I was becoming as sick as those secrets! "Did you get my things back?" I asked my friend upon his return.

"Nobody knows her, and I could not find her anywhere!" he said.

"How could a woman like that just disappear?" I asked, perplexed and somewhat frightened.

"I have no idea, but I asked as much as I could and figured I better get back before they started wondering why I was there," my friend replied. It seemed odd, and I hated to have to go to town to make a new identification and purchase a new stick, but soon I was back to the daily grind and pushed this out of my mind.

A few months later, word came to me that Tamar, my daughter-in-law, was pregnant and that she became that way from the act of prostitution. I was livid! How dare this girl, one who had been married to two of my sons no less, stoop to engaging in sexual relation with someone she did not even know. How embarrassing to our family to know that she had done something of this nature.

Yes, I was the world's greatest hypocrite! I had a very different standard for myself than I did for others. In fact, I often felt better about my own lack of integrity by remaining focused on the shortcomings of those around me. I publicly chastised her and led the charge in demanding her execution for her sinful act.

Feeling smug, I knew that justice was about to be served when all of a sudden, some men yelled for me to come hear what Tamar was saying. As they dragged her out of her home, she was carrying a walking stick and a seal. Someone said that she was saying that the man who she had sex with while acting as a prostitute was the man whom these items belonged to. No way! This could not be happening. I was beside myself. She could not have been that woman with the veil that day, but there was no other explanation. My secret was exposed, and I had nowhere to run.

One of my friends suggested we kill her quickly and tell everyone that she had stolen my goods and was trying to blackmail me. I momentarily gave this some thought. The cries to kill her were becoming louder, but the facts flashed before my eyes. I had refused to let her have my youngest son. I had stooped to seeing prostitutes. I had lied and deceived my daughter-in-law with false promises. I had slept with her and fathered her son. Then a faint memory began to haunt me—that I was also the guy who had betrayed his brother, deceived his father, and spent my life running from their memory. With Tamar about to be killed, I did one of the fastest personal inventories in history.

"Stop!" I yelled to those about to throw her into the fire. "Stop! She is right, and I am more at fault than she is. Let her go!" I don't know if it was the fact that my secret was out or the thought that I had another child who was about to die, along with my daughter-in-law, but I had to stop this from happening. I had to face reality, as humiliating as this was. I had to face the truth and stop running, and this was my chance.

This was my wake-up call. As I grabbed Tamar by the hand and led her away, I suddenly didn't care what anyone else thought. It was time to do the next right thing regardless of how many wrong things were behind me. All I could do was beg her for forgiveness and try to begin a new life.

It was time that I reach out to my dad and my brothers to see how they were doing. It was time that I began to make amends for the way I had treated them and distanced myself after our betrayal of Joseph. Things were not going any better in their farming community than they were in mine. We heard that the Egyptians had plenty of grain in store, thanks to the foresight of some new leader that had been promoted. As we talked, it was agreed that we would go and purchase some grain. While this would be very humbling, we had no other options. As for me, I had come to learn that being humbled is not the worst thing to happen. I was learning to live with a freedom within that was far greater than the bondage and guilt that used to bind my soul.

We were soon standing before a leader in Egypt who held our future in his hands. He could sell or refuse to sell what we needed in order to avoid starvation for our families. He appeared angry and gruff. We stood before him ready to leave when he began asking some of the most prying questions. "Do you have any other brothers?" "Is your father still alive?" (Genesis 43:7) I wondered if he was just being friendly, but soon it was apparent that there was more going on. He sometimes paused as if to gain composure.

He now was demanding that we bring our youngest brother, Benjamin, with us next time or else we would not be able to purchase food any more. My dad's face flashed before me the minute he said this. How would Dad ever agree to something like this after believing that Joseph was already dead? This Egyptian leader then took one of our brothers, Simeon, and said he was holding him until we all came back with Benjamin.

Upon returning to our father, my heart ached for him in seeing how he genuinely feared losing another son. I had been an integral part of betraying Joseph and deceiving our father. Now I was determined that making amends meant doing whatever it took to take responsibility for the predicament we were in and to reassure my dad that nothing would happen to Benjamin. I told Dad that I would take personal responsibility for Benjamin and that if anything happened, he could hold me responsible. I heard my own words and thanked God for the change that he was doing within me. Instead of running from my responsibilities, I was embracing them. Instead of fearing reality, I was facing it head-on. After a few days of wavering, Dad reluctantly agreed, acknowledging that we would all die of starvation if we did nothing. It was agreed; Benjamin was going with us.

We had no illusions upon returning to the Egyptian storehouses. We hoped and prayed that someone else would sell us grain this day. Having the money returned in our sacks, we did not know if we would be accused of stealing, or if we would be given our brother back. We were taken into the Egyptian leader's home. Things got even stranger. We were served a feast. They gave Benjamin the most food. The old me would have been beside myself with jealousy. Instead, I was genuinely happy for Benjamin. He was the youngest and still had a growing appetite. He had been through a lot after losing his brother Joseph. He deserved a break.

Things seemed to go better than we had hoped. Simeon had been released, we had grain in our sacks, and we were on our way again at last. We had barely gotten far down the road when chariots and angry soldiers flagged us down. What now? What could this be about? They accused us of taking the governor's cup. We vehemently denied this, but when they tore into each sack, there it was—in Benjamin's sack, of all places! "This young man is coming with us!" they said. "And the rest of you can go home." How ironic that the only full brother of Joseph, whom we had sold as a slave, was now about to be falsely accused and taken as a slave as well. We would not go home without Benjamin, we explained. If Benjamin was being taken back to the palace, we were all going back to the palace.

As we stood once again before the man who held our lives and our futures in his hands, I did not hesitate. With God's help, and motivated by a heart that had been changed, I stood up and spoke clearly. I would give my own life for the sake of my brother's. If they would send Benjamin home to our father, I would stay and serve out whatever sentence that was called upon. Though I cannot say I was not afraid, I can honestly say that it felt good to do the right thing. Perhaps I would never be able to see Joseph in this life and make amends for what I had done to him, but I could at least stand up for Benjamin and do right by my father. I was not going back without Benjamin!

Somehow this seemed to be all he could take, and the man standing before us sent everyone else out of the room. He began to weep, took off his Egyptian headgear, and spoke to us gently.

"I am Joseph!" he stated. Our heads were spinning. We were speechless. We waited for words of condemnation and revenge, for anger and incrimination. We would deserve every word of it. Instead, we were met with grace. Before we could even offer a word of remorse, he was comforting and embracing us. What we had meant as wrong, God had taken and turned into something good. It was all part of a greater plan, and our brother forgave us! I was overwhelmed. Hearing Joseph's words of forgiveness gave me a renewed sense of hope. If Joseph could see this as part of something bigger, if Joseph could forgive us, then perhaps God could forgive me as well. From that day forward, I lived with a sense of peace. My heart began to heal. I now knew that not only was forgiveness possible, but forgiveness was a reality. It was my reality! My family moved to Egypt. My dad had a new lease on life! I truly am blessed, and in his grace and mercy, God has begun a legacy of redemption and restoration to my family. Thank you for letting me share!

Questions for Reflection:

1. How would you feel if you had a sibling who was given preferential treatment and he seemed to relish his position?
2. What do you think led Judah to the point of rationalizing that somehow it was OK for him to seek out a prostitute?
3. What do you think was the beginning of Judah's repentance and restoration?
4. How do you think Judah felt in realizing he was standing in front of the brother he knew he had betrayed?
5. Have you ever received the kind of forgiveness that Judah experienced from Joseph? What was that like?

6. Can you think of someone that you have hurt and that you need to make amends to or seek reconciliation with?

Principles for Recovery:

1. When you seek to hurt others, you will ultimately hurt yourself.
2. Attempts at revenge against one person leave collateral damage for others.
3. God is able to take your greatest mistakes to serve a larger purpose.
4. Grace is a powerful motivator for transformation.
5. The secrets you keep reveal the heartaches you hide.

A Codependent Leader Avoids Burnout

(Moses's Story)

I am a grateful follower of the Lord God Almighty, and I struggle with low self-esteem, impulsive anger, and codependency. My name is Moses.

Much of my low self-esteem probably began when those who I thought were my brothers and sisters in the palace of Pharaoh began to call me a slave boy and made fun of me for having Hebrew parents. It was hard to know who I was or where I fit in, especially when the lady I thought was my mom sat me down and told me that it was true that I was adopted. As much as she tried to reassure me that she had chosen me and loved me, there was a hole inside of me. I was haunted with questions about my biological family and whether I really belonged in this royal family with a king as a grandfather. I had often felt as if the others did not understand me and had always wondered why, until that moment.

Sometimes as we ventured out beyond the palace walls and walked the streets of our beautiful city, I would admire the great structures. My adopted grandfather was a genius in the building programs he had come up with for our country! Pyramids—what a novel concept! Sometimes my chest swelled with pride over being part of that family. What power, what prestige, and what a heritage I had been adopted into! Yet as I looked closer, the people doing the work did not appear to be enjoying themselves.

Some were being yelled at and driven like animals. This was not right!

I could not believe the first time that I saw one of my adopted people beating one of the Hebrew slaves with a whip, and just because he was working a little too slow and getting behind on an unrealistic quota that had not been met. I swear that that man looked familiar, and I began to wonder if it could be my biological brother that I had heard about. I think that I felt some sense of guilt for having escaped that same treatment. I was escorted around by servants who fed me what I wanted and took me anywhere my heart desired to go, while the rest of my biological family lived in fear of beatings and survived on meager rations of food. I would try to push this out of my mind when back at the palace, but sometimes I avoided going out because of how that made me feel.

Between nagging guilt, painful denial, and helpless feelings of depression, I grew up torn between what I saw outside of the palace and what I enjoyed inside. The more I grew and learned about the real world, the more I struggled with feelings of not belonging in this bubble of privilege. The more I wondered how my real family was coping and what they thought of me living in luxury while they led a life of oppression and abuse, the less I could enjoy what I had.

About this time, I began to struggle with anger. It began with an intense frustration over what I saw and a helplessness to control it. Even when I tried to stay in the palace and not think about what was happening outside, I would hear the cursing of my relatives, the belittling of my family, and the laughing at the predicament of my people. The more I heard, the more I recalled my own painful childhood of being taunted and ridiculed, and the angrier I became. I began to fantasize what I would do and how I would take action if I ever saw someone else being hurt or abused. While I never stood up for myself and tried to ignore the laughter toward me as a child, I began to obsess over how

I could make a difference for someone else, and I daydreamed about that moment when I would help bring justice to this world of unfairness.

I began to venture out of the palace more frequently. I began to relate to my own birth people. I questioned the rights of my adopted family to treat them in such a manner. As I did so, I wanted to let them know that I cared. I wanted to let them know that they did not have to put up with this. I began to have conversations with them. I expected them to appreciate that someone from the palace was listening to them. Instead, they acted like I did not understand and even laughed at the idea that someone walking around in royal robes and sleeping in a palace would care, let alone understand their predicament! How I longed to let them know I was one of them. How I longed for anyone to see me as one of them! I did not fit in anywhere.

My lowest point was the day I came face-to-face with my anger in the harsh face of an Egyptian guard. He was mercilessly beating a Hebrew slave. What was meant to be a punch to rescue the oppressed became a pummeling where I was out of control. My pent-up anger got the best of me, and I was unable to control what was being unleashed. In that moment I released all the unspoken rage at the injustices I had seen and heard. That guard represented every evil face of abuse and oppression that I had ever witnessed and every bully that I had personally faced but not been able to control.

Before I realized what was happening, he lay lifeless on the ground, and a crowd formed. "He killed the guard! He wouldn't stop hitting him," they yelled. I couldn't believe my eyes. I had never been in a fight, let alone murdered someone. I tried to blend into the crowd and disappear as quietly and quickly as possible. I had to lay low, but surely at least the Hebrews would see that they now had a defender and hero to look up to. I felt a blend of being empowered but also of shame and regret. This man also had a family that now had no father and no husband to come home to them that night.

I had crossed a line. I could not return to the palace. I was a wanted man. I found a place to stay with the Hebrews that night and felt that I was safe with my people for once. Perhaps my identity was now with them. The next day I went for a walk and ran across two Hebrew slaves getting into an argument. When I tried to intervene, they immediately jumped on me. Was I going to kill one of them like I had the Egyptian? Who did I think I was, trying to judge them? It became apparent that they did not appreciate my help. My drive to fix the problems of others had now become a problem for me!

After traveling for what felt like forever, I believed I was far enough removed from Egypt to settle down. I stopped to take a rest at a well. I was determined to stay out of trouble, to lay low, and to begin a quiet life nearby. I was unsure of where to begin, who to approach for a place to sleep, and how to choose a livelihood. After spending your whole life in a palace, you don't exactly know a lot of trades! I was deep in thought, just sitting by the well and resting. Soon seven women were there trying to get water for their flock of sheep. Some male shepherds began to bully them and push in front of them. While I had determined to lay low, I could not help but get involved. Injustice seemed to be everywhere. This was not right. I stepped up and told the men to leave these women alone. Perhaps it was because of my Egyptian robes of royalty that I was still wearing, or perhaps it was my pent-up anger at the injustices I had already seen, but they seemed to know I was serious. They backed off and allowed the women the chance to get water to their sheep. I was glad to see them leave, but once again my anger scared me as I knew how close we came to blows.

I sat there for hours, still contemplating my next move. The women returned. One of them, Zipporah, caught my eye. What a gorgeous young woman with a beautiful smile and peaceful look in her eyes. Wait a second; she was coming my way and talking to me. Apparently their dad was upset with them for not inviting me for dinner to thank me for looking out for them. I wasn't expecting this, especially after the response I received when trying to help the Hebrews. Did I have any plans for the evening? Was I new in town, and did I need a place to stay? Thankful for the unexpected invitation and provision, I was soon living with this spiritual man and his family and this beautiful young woman was given to be my wife! Maybe there was a God afterwards! Maybe he had not forgotten me! Perhaps I was being given a second chance at life.

While I still felt reluctant to approach God due to the mistakes I had made, not to mention the long-standing feelings of not belonging anywhere, my heart did begin to soften over time. I had long given up on the idea that my biological people would want anything to do with me or that I could help them in any way. My savior complex had given way to a more passive approach to life and conflict. I did long to know God and admired how my father-in-law spoke of him. It was somewhat different than how I heard the Hebrews do so, and it was definitely different than the religion I saw practiced in the palace of Egypt.

While still unsure of who God was or how to even speak to him, I had a strange experience one day while out watching sheep. Yes, I had learned a trade. It was not a difficult trade, and it certainly allowed me to lay low and not have to deal with people. Sheep were far more peaceful and cooperative than people! Suddenly I saw a glow and felt a sensational warmth. Had someone set a fire to some of the old brush pile across the field? In moving closer, I saw that it was a fire coming from a perfectly green bush. As I was contemplating this strange occurrence, things only got more peculiar. A voice, which left no doubt in my mind as being that of God himself, spoke to me out of the bush. It appeared that the bush on fire was simply a way to get my undivided attention. You never know how God will get your attention. This was how he got mine.

The only thing more shocking than a voice coming from a burning bush was what the voice had to say. He called my name. "Moses, Moses," he said. There is something emotional about hearing God call your name! I knew immediately that it was God even though I can't say that I had ever heard God talking out loud before. I also was extremely frightened. After all, God and I had not had a lot of conversations. I had felt too guilty for what I had done in Egypt to really approach God in any personal way. I definitely had a healthy respect for God and took my sandals off immediately. I also hid my face from fear and shame. But instead of telling me how disappointed he was in me for killing the man in Egypt or from running and leaving my people behind, God was now telling me that he had heard the cries of my people. In fact, in thinking about how to help them, God was saying that he thought I should be the one to go and confront Pharaoh and get our people out of there.

I did not make things easy for God. I told him that there was no way that I could confront Pharaoh. After all, I had a history with his family; and now with my mom out of the picture and my grandfather deceased, the new leadership had no reason to go easy on me, particularly if they remembered the charges against me! Furthermore, I let God know that people would probably laugh at me and not hear anything I had to say. Despite this, God showed some amazing miracles that he could help me perform to convince them. I quickly pointed out that there was a problem with his choice because I cannot talk well, and I neither had any experience in public speaking nor did I have any interest in developing that skill. So much for that fear of God that I initially felt when seeing the bush.

I was pretty bold with God at this point and made it very clear that I was not interested in the position of saving our people. Despite the frustrations he was feeling with my response, God continued to speak calmly. "Fine," he said. My brother, Aaron, could be the spokesperson, and all I had to do was show up and perform the signs and lean on Aaron to do the talking. In fact, he said that he already had Aaron headed my way so we could talk this over right away. Sounds like God had an idea all along of how I was going to respond and already had a plan in place to accommodate my insecurities, my lack of faith, and my lack of confidence.

In case you have not picked up on this by now, I struggled with low self-esteem. Some of this related, no doubt, to my identity issues in childhood and not belonging. It was then compounded by my failure to be accepted by the Hebrews when I tried to be an advocate. Soon I had determined that it was best for me to go about my business and to try and blend in with my new chosen identity—the people of Midian. Getting married, having a job, and raising kids in the community was all helping me begin to feel comfortable—until God showed up and changed all of that. Now I was being stretched far beyond my wildest dreams!

It was a growing process, but God was right about helping me speak. I started out letting Aaron do the talking, but soon we were both doing the talking; and after a while, I took over the role of spokesperson and was doing what God had intended all along. Interesting how God works with us and is patient with our shortcomings but also knows how to get us where he wants us to be!

One of my struggles that I continued to deal with as I began my ministry was that of wanting to keep everyone happy. I did not like conflict. I had enough of that in my early years. Even in my marriage, I had gone along with my wife in some areas where I felt God challenging me to maintain my Hebrew identity.

We did not circumcise our son even though this was the common practice of Hebrews and signified our devotion to God. It took a divine intervention of God, and my wife was still not happy with me or with the idea. She was furious. So much for keeping her happy! Looking back, it would have gone a lot better if instead of avoiding the issue, I had been assertive and proactive enough to explain things and just taken the lead. Because of my passivity, my family did not yet understand this teaching or for that matter many others that I had failed to pass on to them.

As far as keeping others happy, it would not take long to realize that this was simply not possible! For a while it seemed that the leaders of Israel were on board. When they heard what we were trying to do and saw God perform signs, they were impressed. Once they overcame their initial skepticism, we had one beautiful time of worship and prayer. As soon as Pharaoh turned up the heat on them, however, and told the slave drivers to work them harder and make them get their own straw for bricks, the foremen were looking for Aaron and me, and they were anything but pleased! They blamed us for giving the Egyptians an excuse to kill them.

So began years and years of complaints intermingled with times of gratitude and praise by people who looked to me for leadership but also would look at me when needing someone to blame, when things did not happen as expected or hoped for. Yes, God got us out of Egypt and out of slavery, and there were some tremendous shouts of joy when the Red Sea opened and the waters swallowed the enemy. But it was hard hearing people talk as if they were better as slaves in Egypt whenever the journey was taking too long or food became scarce.

One low point for me was when we were in the wilderness, and people were once again in a panic over running out of water. I was not in a great state emotionally. My sister had just passed away. Though constantly focused on the emotions of others, I was never too good at acknowledging my own needs. When they started doubting and complaining (again), God told me to command the rock to produce water. I didn't feel like talking to a rock or for that matter to anyone. I was angry. How many times would it take for these rebels to trust God? How dense could they be? How unappreciative they were over all that we had done for them!! With those emotions raging inside, I grabbed the rod in my hand and hit that rock as hard as I could, twice in a row. Once again, rage had taken over.

While water did gush out of the rock, I had some severe consequences for my actions and loss of control. Since I had not obeyed God, I was now told that I would not be able to actually accompany my people all the way into the promised land and that someone else would have that privilege. What a blow and what a lesson for me in why I need to surrender my will to God's control, not mine.

A turning point in my recovery from codependency occurred when my father-in-law showed up while I was busily going about normal leadership duties in the wilderness. Because I knew that my important duties would not allow me to spend time with my family, I had sent my wife and kids to stay with my in-laws; and after a long period apart, they all arrived in the wilderness. While I took the time to go and greet them upon their arrival, I quickly went back to my duties the next morning and worked long and hard hours, helping solve numerous problems among my people throughout the day. I found a sense of identity in doing so, although the weight of it all became heavy at times. I actually thought that my father-in-law would be impressed by what he saw. His daughter had married an important man whose wisdom and counsel was in great demand! My confidence was tied to what I did, and I was hopeful that I was now living a life of significance.

Just as I was imagining what he would say and how he would be impressed by my performance, I was shocked to hear him say, "This is not good what you are doing!" Had I heard him wrong? What did he mean? He went on to say that working so hard and trying to help everyone in my own strength and wisdom would not only burn me out, but that it was not fair to others. He proposed I set up a structure that would allow others to handle many of the cases and that I share the load. Interesting. While this was a blow to my ego and not at all what I was expecting, it was just what I needed.

I had come to see myself as indispensable. I thought I had to do it all myself. I could not ask others for help and felt like it was all up to me! God used my father-in-law to save my ministry and my sanity. It was not easy, but I began to let go. I began to let others help, and I began to realize that God was not limited to me but had many others who could contribute to what he wanted to accomplish in the community.

Looking back, I am grateful for this man who was willing to confront me on my issues. I am thankful that God was patient with me throughout this process. I went from feeling that I was the hope for saving my people to feeling like a failure who could not even speak for my people. Over time, I had started taking on the burdens of others and was enabling their dependence on me.

With God's help, I now have come to see that I have a role to play in helping my people, but that I am not their savior. I have gifts to offer and I am valuable, but I also have limitations, and do not have to carry this weight alone. I can ask for help. I even allowed two close confidants to help hold up my hands one time when I needed help interceding for my people during an intense battle.

I have legitimate emotions and needs. I have learned to spend some time away, alone on the mountain when I need it. I can tell God exactly how I feel, and he hears me every time. I grieve my losses without losing myself. I keep my anger in check even when others misunderstand me or don't appreciate me like I think they should. God is not finished with me yet, but I am growing. I am learning to ask for help, and I am thankful for all of my identity issues and confusion and struggles in my childhood because it was through those challenges and failures that I have become the man I am today. Thank you for letting me share my story!

Questions for Reflection:

1. How did Moses struggle with two different identities? Share if you have had similar experiences in your childhood.
2. Can you relate to feeling out of place or misunderstood? If so, share your experience with the group.
3. Describe what you think it must have been like for Moses to lead so many people through the wilderness.
4. Why do you think Moses hit the rock when God said to speak to it? How could he have avoided this reaction?
5. How did God use his father-in-law to challenge Moses in his codependency?
6. Who has God used to confront you and to help you face your issues?

Principles for Recovery:

1. When you give up trying to be God, you can begin serving God.
2. You can sometimes help more by helping less.
3. If you don't deal with your emotions within, you won't be able to control your actions without.
4. You can help more people when you allow more people to help you.

A Prostitute Joins the Family

(Rahab's Story)

Some have included me in the list of bad girls in the Bible. Many call my occupation the oldest profession in the world. It was never something I was proud of, but it was also fairly accepted in my culture and had been all I knew for many years. In my day, people said I was a harlot. When they referred to me, it was never just "Rahab" but always "Rahab, the harlot." Today you would call me a prostitute. Thankfully, God calls me his redeemed, restored, and righteous child. I am a grateful believer, and my name is Rahab.

People said I was beautiful. Some ranked me as one of the top four beauties of my time.

It was certainly a superficial ranking and left me feeling that people only saw me for a pretty face. I wanted to be seen for more. I had not done well in relationships. I didn't expect a lot from men. I came to believe they wanted one thing and one thing only. Men had power.

I determined to use what they wanted for my own advantage and to take charge of my own destiny. Strange how I told myself that I was not being taken advantage of, even as I gave away what they wanted over and over. I knew that our encounters together were superficial, and yet I continued with them. What I wanted was also superficial, but at least I was getting paid, and paid well. The sad truth is that what I did came with a cost greater than meets the eye.

It was costing my self-respect.

While I struggled with my profession, I took pride in the fact that I was different than the ones who walked the streets. I was not as bad, as desperate, or as helpless as "those women" were. I would find ways to compare myself to others "worse" than me to cover my own insecurities and self-condemnation.

Yes, I had been there and done that, but I had now settled into a business that included a place to stay. Men could pay extra for my services or simply stay the night while tending to other business. This gave them a good cover when wives came looking. It also paid well and allowed me to pretend to my family that I had given up prostitution and now just offered a bed and breakfast.

It was this cover, and a great location on the wall of Jericho, that brought two Hebrew spies to my place on a night that would change my life forever.

I had heard of the people of Israel. With so many people passing through, I heard things. Now with the word out that they were just across the Jordan and only a few hours away, you could feel the tension and fear building in Jericho.

No one seemed to be able to explain what had made them so successful in battle despite coming from slavery in Egypt and not being trained in warfare. Rumors were flying lately about these unusual people. Some said they had escaped their Egyptian pursuers by walking through a dry spot in the Red Sea—a dry spot of land that had mysteriously opened just in time, and just as mysteriously, closed in on their pursuers.

Everyone thought they would die in the hot and barren desert, but they had somehow found enough food to eat and sufficient water to drink to sustain their massive numbers. Some credited their success to leadership and mentioned a man named Moses. Others called it luck. Now they had a new leader and still had stories of countless battles in which they were outnumbered and out-skilled and yet still came out victorious.

The theory that caught my attention was the one that said it was the God they believed in who made the difference for these people.

God. Who or what was he anyway? When we talked about a god in my world, it was a local spirit or an image that someone created and declared to be a source of help or a divine good luck charm that helped people to cope with life.

But what I heard about these people suggested that they thought of their God as a being who transcended this life and lived outside of merely one group of people and had created the entire world. Talk was that others were welcomed to join them in worshipping this God. I couldn't help but wish that I knew a being who was real, powerful, able to forgive someone like me, and who cared about my life.

Sometimes that just seemed like wishful thinking.

Now two strange men were here asking for a room for the night. They had heard about my place from travelers who had been to Jericho. They made it clear they were not here for any other services than a place to stay. Then they paused. There was one other thing.

Here it comes, I thought. All men want something. Whatever they wanted, I would need to accommodate them. It was putting my reputation at stake not to do so. This was getting so old and felt so empty.

But wait, they were not asking for sexual favors. They wanted information on Jericho and heard I might be able to help. It was true that if there was any information on the people of the city, I knew it. I had customers from all walks of life. People let their guard down around me. I was known to protect their identity and to guard their secrets.

But what did they need this information for, and why were they scoping out our city? If I was to help them, I would need some information as well. What were they planning, and why were they here? It was obvious they were Hebrews from the way they talked and dressed, but what did they want with Jericho?

Reluctantly, looking from side to side, they disclosed their mission. They took a risk in trusting me, and I learned of their intentions to attack Jericho soon. I told them that I had heard amazing things about their people, good things about their ethics, and supernatural stories about their God. They acknowledged it was true and credited this God for their success.

While I was intrigued with their success on the battlefield, I was even more amazed to hear of their God. This sounded like a God who was more than a good luck charm—a God who actually cared about the people who followed him.

"Does your religion accept people from other nations?" I reluctantly asked. "What about people in my profession?"

I had heard that they had higher standards about these matters than the people of Canaan.

"Our God loves all people," they assured me. "And we have provisions for others to participate in worship and for all of us to receive forgiveness. Our ancestor Abraham was told from the beginning that we were to be a blessing to others and that others would find God through us."

It sounded too good to be true. I was talking to the "enemy." *Is there a chance I could join them? Would it do any good to ask? What would I have to lose?* My whole city was about to be attacked, and everything that I knew said that these people would come out on top and that Jericho would be destroyed.

And now my hopes of a new start and a relationship with a God who was real were springing up within me. Any hope that I had of a new life, or potentially any life at all, depended on it. I decided I would ask.

Before I had a chance to say another word, there was banging on the door. It was not someone knocking for a room. This was the type of banging when soldiers came to capture a man who was wanted for deserting his post, or the banging of that wife who knew her husband was here and had come to let him have it.

"Quick!" I told them. "Up to the roof. You will find some flax there. Crawl under it and lay very still."

The flax was part of my plan of escaping this life by making my own linens and selling or trading them. That way I could be free of guilt and proud of the work I did.

I was jolted back to reality as the banging continued. I opened the door to face impatient soldiers demanding answers about spies on the loose.

"Two spies you say?" I spoke out, loudly enough that the spies might hear. "There were a couple of men here earlier who may fit that description, but they left at sundown. If you hurry, you may be able to catch up to them!"

I lied.

"I do hope you find them, and if they come back, I will let you know!" I yelled behind them as they hurriedly took off, exiting Jericho to search the countryside.

I was relieved. We were safe! I had thrown my lot in with the Hebrew spies and knew that their God had brought them here and kept them safe. In fact, I was beginning to wonder if he had also sent them for me.

I had cried out on several occasions that if God was real, he would let me know. I knew that the life I had chosen was empty, and that even though I was trying to change, I did not know how. I felt used but also wanted, and the insanity continued. I needed a power greater than myself to restore me to a semblance of sanity!

I headed up the stairs and onto the roof.

"They are gone, and you will be safe here tonight," I told them.

I then blurted out my growing faith in their God and my amazement of his hand on their people. I told them I was sure that he was the Supreme Being and that he would let them conquer the whole land, including my city of Jericho.

Then, knowing that they now owed me, I spoke quietly but firmly, "Promise me that when you come back, you will spare my life and that of my family."

"If you bring all your family into your house and keep this scarlet rope hanging in your window, and if you don't betray us after we leave, we swear that you and your family will be spared," one of the men said. "But if any of you goes running back into the city, we cannot be responsible for them. Everyone must remain here in this building and wait to be rescued."

"I accept those terms," I replied, then gave them instructions to climb down from my window, across the wall.

I told them to wait a few days in hiding in the woods before venturing back to their camp. By then the soldiers from Jericho would give up the chase, and they would be safe. Yes, I could be bossy at times, and tended to be a strong woman. I have had to be. They followed my advice and soon were out of sight.

Now to convince my family that I was not crazy and that we all needed to let go of any hopes of Jericho winning this upcoming battle. My family was not as close as I had wished they would be. They had reservations about my line of work, but they also were part of my reason for it. There was a lot of dysfunction there, and I was not the first one in the family to make poor choices.

At least they were relieved that I had chosen to locate back in Jericho and close to home. Now they would hopefully appreciate the fact that I had negotiated a future for all of us and not just myself. I tended to be independent but was trying to include others better than I used to. My heart was changing, and maybe this also had to do with God at work in my life.

The next few weeks were filled with a mixture of anxiety and anticipation, fear and faith, guilt and growth! I wondered at night if they were coming back soon. If so, would they remember us and honor their word, a promise to a prostitute? Surely God's hand was in all of this.

I prayed over and over telling him that I was done with my old ways and that I would follow his will for my future. But then customers continued to show up, and what used to be something I excused and felt numb to, now created nagging guilt within. I had to change, but I needed to get away from my old places, people, and things in order to make change work.

One day I woke to shouts up and down the city wall. "They are coming! Prepare to defend Jericho! Secure the wall!"

I rushed out to get my parents, brother, sister, and a few other relatives in town back to my place. We huddled in the back room, by the window on the wall.

The thoughts flew through my head. "What if the soldiers from Jericho see us about to escape and kill us all?"

The "what ifs" began to overwhelm me and I tried to bring my mind back to the "what is."

God has made a promise, and he is faithful to deliver on it. I have a new faith. My family and I are still safe. I needed to stay focused on this and on the moment before me.

We watched as a huge number of people marched around our city. Some strangely dressed men, who I later learned were priests, had a prominent place, guarding a big ark and blowing huge ram horns. Our soldiers stood on the wall, armed with arrows and ready, should they come closer.

Surprisingly, after a full march around the city, they began to retreat back to their camp. Some of my family suggested they were giving up, afraid to fight. I knew better.

The next morning, I heard jeering from some of the men on the wall next door. I woke my family again.

"They are back, and this must be the day," I whispered.

We gathered again by the window. I made sure the scarlet rope was still there, hoping this rope did not raise suspicions of our soldiers or neighbors. Even as our men jeered and taunted the marching Hebrews, nobody yelled back at them. They were eerily silent. The only sound was from our people laughing and making fun and the occasional blowing of the horns.

After six days of this, people on the walls paid less attention to those "crazy Hebrews" marching around. My family members began to doubt my promises and my new found faith. I still believed but also struggled with doubts.

Sometimes when you find faith, it is easy to believe but harder to wait. I knew this God had to be real. I knew that I needed a God who was willing to offer a second chance to someone like me. I knew, but I did not understand.

Why would we have to sit up on this wall day after day, wondering and waiting? Why wouldn't God have delivered us the first day?

Apparently God's ways are not our ways, and God's timing is not our timing. Waiting is not easy, but it does have a way of refining our faith and shaping our character.

The seventh day started like all the others. After that familiar march around the walls, we expected to watch them return to camp just like the other days. This time they did not leave. They went around again and again and again.

Some of them looked tired. Just when I thought they were going to stop, they took up that last momentous march. I wondered if they were about to give up. Even if God tells you to do something, waiting can make you wonder. Did they get this wrong? Was God really going to help give them Jericho?

My questions began as well. How would they get past the soldiers on the wall? This was one of the most protected cities in our region. There was no way under these walls; and to try to get over them, that would be a suicide mission.

My thoughts were interrupted by my dad. "They have stopped," he whispered.

As I huddled with the others by the window, it was true—the entire procession had stopped, as if waiting for something. The priests sounded the horn longer and louder than any time before.

Then this group of seemingly quiet and patient people let out the loudest shout that I heard in all of my life.

All I could hear was crumbling, crashing, and the sounds of my neighbors and soldiers screaming as they ran to get off the walls that were falling quickly. When all was collapsing around me, it would have been easy to run, but I reminded my family to remain calm and to have faith. Even before I could say it again, Hebrew soldiers had come through the window with the rope, let us down, and guided us to freedom.

The soldiers of Jericho were too stunned and too busy running for their lives to notice or to care. We were led to freedom just before everything on the walls tumbled down and the walls themselves fell flat.

With newfound adrenaline, we were led to their camp. The spies came up to me, and I bowed low with gratitude, thanking them for keeping their promise. They introduced me to Joshua, their leader, and a man with him named Salmon, who was apparently a well-respected individual in their community. His kind smile and friendly disposition caught my attention immediately.

The way he looked at me was different than the men I was used to. I wondered, though, how he would feel if he knew what I did for a living.

As I settled in, it turned out that everyone knew my story. A few judged me and a few women kept their distance and made their husbands keep theirs. But amazingly, the ones with the most sincere faith seemed to accept me and chose to include me.

Joshua told everyone to give me a chance and told them of my newfound faith.

The man with the kind and friendly smile and I became better acquainted. Being around him was different than being around other men I knew. He seemed to look beyond the physical and see something of value within me.

One day, he asked me to marry him. Soon we had settled in the new promised land that everyone had been waiting for.

Salmon and I were given some prime real estate in the new land and began a family together. What a proud day when Boaz was born. He was a gentle soul, much like his father, but also had my business sense and my way with people. He grew up showing kindness and concern for all people.

I may be biased, but I thought that our boy was one of the most eligible bachelors in the land. I could not figure out why it took him so long in getting married. One day, he came home and calmly told us about his engagement to Ruth, a woman from Moab, who had converted to our faith.

I realized then that God had used my past and my conversion from outside the faith not only to give me a second chance personally but also to help those around me know that God does not see as man sees.

How many other Hebrew men would have been open to marrying and becoming kinsman redeemer for an outsider? Boaz learned, from our story, that God does not care where you have been, only where you are going. Salmon gave me a chance, and now Boaz was giving that same opportunity to a beautiful widow from Moab who needed it just as much as I had.

No, I did not start well. Many will continue to remember me throughout history as Rahab, the prostitute. That is OK. Sometimes I began to go back there myself. Sometimes I would still hear a voice in my head saying I was not as good as these other people of faith around me.

But God took all of my life, not just the good parts but the broken parts too. He did an unbelievable thing. He decided to bring the Messiah through my great-grandson David.

Apparently God wanted to spell it out loud and clear for all to see. He does not choose us because we have it all together but because we don't! His love sees our need. His grace looks not at what we are coming out of but at what he can change us into. I hope that my story encourages you to look ahead and not back.

When someone continues to declare who you WERE, hold your head up and tell them WHOSE you have BECOME. My name is Rahab, a relative of Jesus Christ, and a valued child of God! Thank you for letting me share.

Questions for Reflection:

1. What is the significance of Rahab being in the line of Christ?
2. How do you think Rahab felt about herself and what she did?
3. What kind of reactions do you think Rahab faced when she joined the people of Israel and they all learned of her history? Have you been welcomed or shunned when you have gone to church?
4. Reflect on God's providential manner in which he saved Rahab and her family. When has he unexpectedly stepped into your life?
5. Rahab took some risks to help the spies. What risks did she take? How have you also had to take risks in trusting people?
6. What do you think Rahab was feeling as she waited for the people of Israel to return? When have you had to wait on God, and what was that like for you?
7. How did God use Rahab and her husband to prepare Boaz to marry Ruth? In what ways do you believe God can use your past for his kingdom in the future?

Principles for Recovery:

1. Don't let shame of the past keep you from hope for the future.
2. If you don't take the risk of change, you won't gain the joy of victory.

3. Fear of the "what ifs" can prevent enjoying the "what is."

4. Sharing your past may help change someone else's future.

From Fear to Faith

(Gideon's Story)

My name is Gideon. I am a believer in God who also struggles with issues of fear, doubt, and a lack of self-esteem.

I was from the tribe of Manasseh, a tribe of little distinction. My family was not very well known either.

Growing up, I had little confidence and few friends. I rarely signed up for community events, not seeing the value in doing so and feeling that I had nothing to contribute. We were farmers—had been for generations. I married several women and had many children—seventy sons and just about as many daughters! It was a busy household, but I was thankful for the help in the fields. We also had a good number of servants helping.

Things were going well until the Midianites showed up.

Our country was weak. We had no real leadership. We had lost our moral compass and even our faith in God. Many of us had given up on the true God, feeling that he had forgotten us. Many had even begun praying to Baal or other gods instead—gods that we could at least see in a tangible form.

The Midianites were cruel. Many of our people began hiding in caves and crevices in the mountains where they could avoid detection. As soon as our crops were planted, raiders from Midian, Amalek, and their allies would show up, camp out, and take what they wanted, destroying the rest.

One time when I saw a band coming, I begged them to take what they desired and leave the rest for us. No such luck; they enjoyed arrogantly parading their power as much as taking our

hard-earned crops that had finally ripened. They helped themselves to our camels, goats, sheep, donkeys, and cattle. There
were too many of them for us to resist. As for myself, I didn't see
the sense in trying. I lived as a captive to fear.

The only thing keeping my family and me from utter starvation was the wheat that I had learned to hide and thresh in the
well-enclosed winepress. One day, I had a close call when I heard
voices outside, but I told my boys and the servants to stop talking
and remain still. Soon the intruders were gone, and all was quiet.

Nobody expected much to be happening in an old winepress,
especially when all the grapes in the entire valley had been con-
fiscated by the Midianites. I was proud of my clever idea, though
also embarrassed that I was cowering in fear. Wheat was meant
to be threshed out in the open, high on the hills, anywhere the
wind could blow, not hidden this way. I simply did what I had to
do to survive. I certainly was not prepared for what I was about
to hear.

I was alone that day, and the voice startled me.

"Mighty hero, the Lord is with you!" (Judges 6:12)

It echoed through the winepress, and I jumped. I soon realized this was a messenger from the Lord. While I had never seen
an angel before, this was clearly no ordinary man, and he brought
no ordinary message.

"If the Lord is with us, why has all this happened to us?"
(Judges 6:13) I questioned. It was hard to accept that God was
with us when the Midianites had all but destroyed our land and
sent us into hiding. So much for all the promises and all the stories of God delivering the people of Israel. I was still in denial of
any personal responsibility of myself or my people despite all of
us abandoning our faith. I saw it the other way around.

"But now, the Lord has abandoned us!" I continued. I let this
angel know that I did not believe that the Lord was with me.
How could he be? Too many bad things had happened in my life

for me to trust this God. Besides, what would he want with me anyway?

Thinking that my negativity and doubts would be more than enough to scare any messenger from God away, I was prepared to go back to the work at hand. He persisted, however, with an even more startling word from God: "Go with the strength you have, and rescue Israel from the Midianites. I am sending you!" (Judges 6:14)

He had to be kidding. *The strength I have? That sure wasn't much! Me, rescue Israel?* I didn't know whether to laugh or to cry. I didn't do either—I simply continued to argue with God.

It wasn't disrespect. I was arguing because I had to let him know that he had the wrong guy! Not only was I the coward who was presently in hiding, I was from a mediocre family with no standing that could command respect. On top of that, I was the least likely of anyone among my siblings to succeed at anything, particularly leading a band of soldiers to fight an enemy like Midian. I saw myself in the light of my fears and failures; God apparently saw me in the light of my potential and my future.

"I will be with you, and you will destroy the Midianites as if you were fighting against one man!" he reassured me. (Judges 6:16)

For some, that may have been all that was needed. For a guy who had never won a fight against even one man, and who trembled at the thought, it was still not enough. I needed reassurance. I needed a sign. I also realized that if I was to even consider serving this God that I had neglected for so long, I needed to prepare an offering.

"Wait here, and don't go away until I come back and bring my offering to you," I said.

"I will be here when you return," he answered.

I hurried. I was starting to get hopeful. I was still anxious, however, and unsure what would happen. With a small but growing faith welling up inside, I went home, cooked one of the few goats that had not been taken by the Midianites, grabbed some freshly baked bread and a pot of soup, and returned to find the angel still sitting there, waiting.

God is so patient, so much more patient with me than I have ever been with him.

When I did as I was told, placing the food upon a rock, the most amazing thing happened. A fire shot up from the rock and consumed the entire offering of food, and the angel disappeared. This is when I realized I had been talking to more than just a messenger. I had been talking to God himself.

From that point in my life, I no longer had to have a messenger to talk to God. I built an altar to God in order to show my faith and surrender to him. Then and there I committed my life and will to him the best I knew how. I now knew that he had never left me, but I had abandoned and neglected him. He had always wanted a relationship with me. I was now ready to listen.

I was still a work in progress, however—fearful, though determined. God told me that I needed to get rid of some idols that our family had put in place. Idols can be anything we choose to worship other than the true Creator and Supreme Higher Power. For some people, this can be an addiction, another individual in their life, or their own desires and material pursuits.

For our family, it was an altar to Baal and an Asherah pole erected to honor Asherah, another poor substitute for the true God I had now come to believe. Once destroying these false idols, I was instructed to prepare an altar to God, using as fuel the very wood from the Asherah pole. Even in this simple command, God was reassuring me that he could even take my poor choices and mistakes of the past and use them as fuel for my future and for his glory.

Being the "brave" man that I was, I decided that the best time to follow these instructions would be when nightfall came and most people would be sleeping. With ten of my strongest and bravest servants to help, we carried out our mission.

As darkness lifted and the men of town moved about, the destruction of the old altars and establishment of the new was soon evident to all. With a little detective work, they discovered that we were responsible and went straight to my dad's place to demand that he turn me over for a sentence of death.

I waited, trying to catch my breath, and wondered how my dad would handle the mob before him. Dad, the one who had erected those idols in the first place, surprised me with his response and made me very proud. He had obviously had a change of heart as well.

"If Baal truly is a god, let him defend himself and destroy the one who broke down his altar!" he stated as he turned and went back into the house. (Judges 6:32)

As much as I credit Dad with quieting down the mob, I knew it was God who had given him this wise response. It was also God who had gotten the community's attention, and now everyone knew that I, Gideon, was ready to take on all those who opposed the God of Israel.

As the armies of Midian, Amalek, and their partners from the east assembled to oppose us, God gave me courage. I went out with a ram's horn and made the call to arms. Yes, I was stepping up not because I had a great track record of faith or even courage, for that matter, but because God had assured me that all he needed was this little bit of strength and faith that I did have and that he would then do the rest.

I wish I could say I never looked back and never doubted or questioned God again. That would not be accurate, however. Once again, as we got closer to battle, my doubts crept in, and my insecurities mounted.

Had I really heard God right? Was he really going to do this and use me? I had learned, though, in this newfound walk with God that he could handle my doubts, so I went ahead and let him know exactly what I was feeling and asked him for reassurance.

God was gracious. He did not get angry, even after I asked again. I am thankful for a God who is patient with my doubts and insecurities. Without that, I would not be standing here today.

Reassured that he was indeed with me, I rallied the troops. Thirty-two thousand volunteered. It was heartwarming and encouraging to see so many men standing before me ready to fight!

"That's too many," God told me. "Whoever is timid or afraid may leave this mountain." (Judges 7:2-3)

I wanted to ask God if that included me. I knew better though. Now, despite some lingering fear, I knew that I did not want to go back to a dull life of fearful hiding. I wanted to be part of what God was about to do.

After letting the men know that God was OK with a smaller number and giving them permission to sit this one out, twenty-two thousand left, leaving us a small army of ten thousand.

"Are you sure this is enough?" I asked the Lord.

"Actually," he replied, "there are still too many."

God wanted to make sure that when this victory was won, we knew why. Even when we pray and ask for his help, it is common for us to turn around and think that we pulled it off in our own strength. To that end, he gave me further instructions, as random as they seemed, that would bring down our number to a small band of three hundred. Three hundred men about to take on an alliance of 135,000. This definitely would have to be God's doing!

If the number was unconventional, the military strategy was going to be even more so. As we waited one more night to attack, I was again struggling with fear. God was patient.

"Gideon, I have given you victory over them, but if you are afraid to attack, go down to the camp and listen to what the Midianites are saying, and you will be greatly encouraged."

God even told me who to take with me. He did not want me to be alone in my struggle. We do better when we have supportive individuals who walk with us in our journey, especially when we are wavering. Sure enough, we heard just what we needed to hear and knew that God had prepared this moment. He had given the enemies a dream that struck fear in their hearts and brought courage to ours.

With our loud horns, breaking pots, and unified shouts of confidence in God, we startled a sleeping camp. Then lifting our torches high in the air, we stood there watching God fight the battle as men scurried from their tents and began attacking each other, dazed and unsure of who or where their enemy was.

Many ran, without looking back. Then I notified the men of the tribes they were running to, and they joined in the chase. The Midianites were defeated. The Israelites knew that God had given them victory. The two leading commanders were captured and killed, one by a winepress, of all places. How ironic! God used a man who had fearfully hidden in a winepress to lead an army who would in turn kill an enemy general hiding in the same manner.

While God made it clear that this victory came from his power and not our own, he also made it clear that he had a role for us to play if we would only step up to the plate. We had to show up and be available for the battle. We had to prepare the clay pitchers, horns, and torches.

Once the initial victory was in place, we had to chase down those who were not destroyed in the camp. Fifteen thousand of the 135,000 had escaped and still had to be tracked down.

I also learned that I had to keep my eyes on God and not on people. Even the people who are supposed to be on your side can stand in the way. Many of the people in towns we passed through refused to feed us as we hunted down the remaining enemies. I also had some of the guys in Ephraim upset because they didn't get to be in on the first part of the battle.

Thankfully, God helped me not to take their comments personally and gave me the words to say to calm their anger. He gave me humility to assure them that they had more to offer than I ever had. What had been my insecurities and lack of confidence allowed me to humbly build them up, knowing that my security was now in someone bigger, and it didn't matter what they thought of me. I also could see where their anger came from. Much of it stemmed from their own insecurities. Truly, God never wastes a hurt, and he allowed all I had been through to help me relate calmly to men who felt overlooked and insecure.

I learned a lot on my journey. I finally realized what God meant when he told me to go in the strength I had. He didn't need me to be strong and powerful. He didn't need me to be confident and courageous. He didn't need me to have a great history or a superior family background. He just needed me to be willing to surrender my will to his. He needed me to be available, not able. He was able. He was the power source. I was simply the vessel for the power to flow through.

I also learned I need to be careful. It's easy, when you think you have everything figured out, to believe that you are better off than you really are.

With God's help, Israel was thriving. They even asked me to be king. Fortunately, I had sense enough to decline the offer and tell them that God needed to be their king. I had no ambitions to rule over them.

But I also messed up. Realizing that they would do pretty much anything I asked, I suggested they share some of the gold jewelry that they had plundered from the enemy. There was plenty to go around, and I had a plan. I wanted to build a memorial.

I took the gold that was eagerly collected and made a statue in the middle of town. *Surely this would be a good way for all of us to remember what God had done*, I rationalized. I forgot what a trap any statue could be and how idols quickly form as substitutes to the real God and true Higher Power. Soon, people began worshipping this statue instead of the God it was to represent.

How soon we forget, and how important it is to stay alert to pitfalls of the past.

I hope that as you hear my story, you will be encouraged to know that God doesn't see you the way you see yourself. He wants to use you in the strength that you have, regardless of how little you may think that it is. When you surrender your power, his power will replace yours. He will bring you to victory in whatever you are facing. It does not mean you will never be afraid. I was. But it does mean that he will be with you in your fear and that he will take what little you have and turn it into a victory.

God also wants you to know that he does not need you to have a vast number of people on your side to get you through this. He only needs for you to gather with others who are facing similar battles with similar enemies. Even if it is only you and a few others, please know that the victory is yours not because of how many of you there are or how strong you may feel but because of who has sent you into battle! The power is his, not yours.

When you release control, renounce the doubts, and rely upon him, you will overcome. and you will win the war!

Thank you for letting me share.

Questions for Reflection:

1. Gideon felt like God had abandoned them. Have you been through periods of questioning and wondering where God had gone?
2. Do you ever feel too weak, too small, or too broken for God to use you?
3. Why do you think God chose to use a man who was hiding, fearful, and full of doubts to rescue his people?
4. How do you see Gideon growing in this story?
5. Gideon fell into a "trap" toward the end of his life. What are potential traps for your progress and your recovery?

Principles for Recovery:

1. Take responsibility for where you are so God can take you to where you could be.
2. God doesn't see you for where you have been; he sees you for where you can go.
3. You won't experience the victory if you don't engage in the battle.
4. Just because you gave up one idol does not mean you are not vulnerable to another.

Sex, Anger, and Addiction

(Samson's Story)

My story begins with a mom and dad who loved God and adored me, their only child. That is not the typical beginning to a story of addiction, but along with growing up in a godly home and becoming a prophet of God for my people, I also developed a sexual addiction. My name is Samson.

My parents had prayed for me and set me aside as a Nazarite. What that meant was that I was not to drink wine (or have anything to do with grapes), I could not touch dead animals, I could never cut my hair, and I was expected to be dedicated to God in how I lived my entire life. It was not so unusual to commit to thirty days, sixty days, or even ninety days as a Nazarite, but a lifelong Nazarite commitment was considered a bit fanatical and extreme, especially for that time.

I lived in the period of Judges, when truth and morality were relevant, and each person decided what was right. Despite my cultural surroundings, my parents taught me well, and I knew what God expected for me and for my people. My issues did not surface overnight. Little by little, I began to cross boundaries and ignore rules that were set for me.

It was not easy growing up with a different set of rules from everyone else. Mom and Dad told me when I was pretty young that I was set apart for something special and that God had spoken to them about me. Sometimes I wondered what that would be and how God was going to use a kid like me.

Other times, I was angry at the things I had to give up for this commitment.

"No, Samson, you are not allowed to have grapes or drink grape juice."

"I know all your friends are looking for carcasses this weekend, but you are not allowed to touch those."

"I don't care how much they laugh at you; God said not to cut your hair."

It was tough being different.

I was blessed with the gift of unusual strength. I gradually discovered this when others picked at me and I fought back. My strength was not meant to serve myself but to serve others and to glorify God. I had been taught this well. When the teasing became intense, however, I fought back.

By fighting, I thought I would earn respect. I determined never to let others push me around the rest of my life. While God gives gifts, he does not necessarily restrict our misuse of them. This indulgence would get me in trouble for years to come.

As I became a young man, I found that my feats of strength impressed the young ladies. They loved the stories of the wild animals I had killed with my bear hands. When I got into a fight, I may have lost the respect of some, but I gained the respect of others. The godly girls (who were few and far between) respected that I was a Nazarite. They liked the fact that I believed in God and followed him. The ungodly ones, particularly the Philistines, thought this was strange and fanatical. They were also the ones who liked it when I fought back, when I wouldn't take anything from anyone, and when I showed off my strength. They gave me attention that made me feel desirable. Being desired began to be a greater motivation then being respected. Soon, my judgment clouded.

Despite all that I had been taught and the values that I believed, I was making choices that were based on my wants and desires, not my convictions or commitments. Gradually, the rationalizations in my head became more powerful than the reasoning of my parents. The stirrings of my heart to serve God and my people became fainter, and my principles became weaker as I rationalized my choices.

My rationalizations ran something like this:

"At least I am still avoiding alcohol!"

"God created sex to be enjoyed."

"This girl and I really love each other."

"What my parents don't know won't hurt them."

"You should see what everyone else is doing these days!"

On and on the excuses went; and the slide down the slippery slope picked up speed.

One of my early rationalizations had to do with a beautiful Philistine girl who I wanted to marry. At least I was wanting to do the right thing and marry her. My parents were appalled that I would think of marrying someone other than a Jewish girl. I thought they were old-fashioned and perhaps bigoted.

Sure, I knew it was the fact that she worshipped idols and not the true God, but I could tell them that they needed to get with the times. Everyone was doing it. Besides, she looked way better than any of the girls back in my hometown. I let them know that I wanted to marry her, regardless of their objections. I knew they would give in. They always had.

Being an only child and born in their later years after they had tried for years to have a baby, it was easy to manipulate them and get what I wanted. After all, I was God's gift to them and set apart as special—a fact that we all would come to take for granted.

The marriage did not last long, that's for sure! During the wedding festivities, I challenged some men with a riddle, attempting to have some sport and win a wager. They convinced my bride to get the answer out of me. I held off telling her for quite a few days. Once she played the "you don't love me" card, I could not hold back any longer.

Surely she would not betray my secret, but she did.

I became so angry—at her, at them, at everyone, even at myself.

I killed thirty people with that reckless rage just to get what I had promised to pay my debt from the wager. Then, when I simmered down enough that I thought I could go make love to my wife, it was too late.

Her dad had married her off to the best man at my wedding. All I had wanted was to be with this beautiful woman. Now she was no longer mine. This angered me so much I went off and devised a plan of revenge. It was not easy catching three hundred foxes, but when I did, I tied their tails together, lit them on fire, and turned them loose to ravage the fields of the Philistines.

After all, it served them right. That was not enough for me, however; I hid out in a cave and went on killing sprees to attack all the Philistines I could after this. One day I killed one thousand men in a single day—with a jawbone of a donkey, no less! I felt fearless and powerful.

Living in a cave was somewhat symbolic of my life. I had come to live with certain secrets and isolation from others. I was not close to others. Most of us who struggle with sexual addiction are not. I was so used to keeping secrets that I withheld a lot.

Even when the coolest thing happened, and I killed a lion with my bear hands, I didn't tell anyone. Then when I found the carcass full of bees and honey, I even took the honey to my parents but never told them where I got it.

After all, I had just violated another of my Nazarite vows in touching a carcass. Oh well. My attitude was becoming more calloused to the boundaries I crossed. Keeping secrets kept a distance between myself and others.

I was not close to anyone really. Even when I got married, the best man was another Philistine whom I hardly knew. The more I keep secrets, the more I felt alone; and the more I felt alone, the more I kept secrets.

Keeping secrets soon allowed me to cross another boundary. I never thought I would stoop to seeing a prostitute. My previous indiscretions were more "respectable" in nature. Each indiscretion and violation of my commitment to God was disturbing, but this one would take it to a new level. As I said, I was on a slippery slope, and I could not stop this downward slide. Seeing prostitutes became a way for me to deal with my loneliness and isolation.

One day, when people saw me going in to see a prostitute in the town of Gaza, they thought they had me cornered and locked me into the town and slept nearby waiting to attack me in the morning. Something told me to get out of there early.

Maybe it was God protecting me, despite where I was. Maybe it was my own sense of guilt that stirred me to leave. I left at midnight, while the men were still asleep. When I got to the town gate, I used my gift of strength to tear it down. I then carried that big old gate, beams and all, right up on my shoulders, uphill, all the way out of the city.

You would think that all of those close calls would teach me a lesson. Surely after being deceived by one woman and being set up by others, I would stay out of trouble.

Hardly. They say that insanity is doing the same thing over and over and expecting a different outcome. Once again, in the midst of a relational void and absence of any deep walk with God, I was looking for pleasure and companionship in all the wrong places. This time it was with Delilah.

With Delilah things felt different. We actually cared for each other; I thought. It was more than just a physical attraction, and I saw her more than once. Soon we were enough of an item that without my knowing it, some men in the community were conspiring with her against me, knowing that I would be there again and again.

My problem, after spending so much time in isolation and so little time in real community, was that I did not know who to trust. In fact, I usually erred on the side of not trusting anyone. My infatuation with Delilah, however, led me to ignore my instincts and overlook the red flags.

She asked me to share what made me strong. Just in case, I did not tell her the real source, the symbol of my long hair and God giving me strength due to my vows to him. It did feel good to have her asking though, and after all, I did not think she would ever know the difference. She just wanted to get to know me better, right?

Somehow the very night that I had misled her by saying my strength could not withstand being tied down with seven bow strings, some men came in and attacked me. Of course, I snapped free immediately. Delilah said they overpowered her and she could not keep them out and that they had tied me up.

Strange timing, I thought.

She told me how betrayed she felt that I had lied to her. Soon, I found myself making up another story—how it really had to be brand new ropes. That same night that I told her this, they showed up again and I broke free with ease. Once again, she told me that she could not stop them and that she had felt betrayed that I lied to her. While beginning to feel suspicious of Delilah, my infatuation for her and desire to be with her caused me to overlook the dangers. I also felt bad about deceiving her.

This time when she asked, I got closer to the truth, and I told her that it was related to my hair, but I still lied and said all she had to do was braid my hair and I would become powerless. The truth was that I was already powerless. I was powerless over my compulsive behaviors and my addiction to needing a beautiful woman to help me gain a false sense of value. I was a powerless man who used illusions of strength to avoid the real issues in my life.

The strange thing about addiction is that you may know better and even vow not to repeat the same stupid choices yet still find yourself right back in the same place. While I was on guard for a little bit after these experiences with her, especially after it became obvious that she was the one who braided my hair in my sleep, I somehow began to weaken again.

She told me that she was only wanting to be sure I was being honest with her and that I loved her enough to tell her the truth. She told me she did not feel that I really loved her or that I would tell her everything. Well, I certainly did not want to lose her. I really loved being around her. As she pointed out, no Philistines had come around the last few times I was there. Maybe I could trust her with the truth. She swore that she would never tell a soul and that she just wanted to know me better.

Maybe it was safe to try one more time. Maybe this time there would be a different outcome. She vacillated between pleading, crying, nagging, and sometimes demanding. She eventually wore me down.

Yes, insane as it was, and as many times as I have relived that moment in my head, I told her everything. I told her about the hair. I told her about God and about my being a Nazarite. She looked a little surprised about that, perhaps because of all that we were involved in together. I know that she also had heard of my past with other women.

But I told her all, and she showered me with appreciation. She knew that I had finally told her the truth. As I lay there, I hoped that I had done the right thing. Surely she was not going to betray me, and surely this would satisfy her, and we would be together now for a long time. Maybe she was the one I was to spend my future with. Maybe everything would now be OK. With these thoughts and hopes, I found myself drifting off to sleep.

Once again, she lulled me to sleep in her arms, and once again I was awakened to men coming in to try and take me away. I struggled in vain, however. I had never felt so powerless, so weak.

What happened? I wondered.

I could not move, could not resist, and could not stop them from dragging me out of the house. I saw locks of hair laying on the floor—long locks of hair. Surely she had not done this to me. As I was dragged away, I saw one of the men paying Delilah, and I realized the truth. I had been taken in and betrayed.

Delilah had given me up for monetary gain. Now I was not only powerless to resist her clutches, but I was powerless literally. I soon found it useless to try and resist these men who became my captors and tormentors.

I awoke in shackles early the next morning and was marched in front of the Philistine leaders. I had no idea what they had planned for me other than making fun and having the last laugh.

I saw the man who had briefly been my father-in-law, upon whom I had taken revenge. I saw the family members of a man who had been part of the thousand I killed with a jawbone. I heard the laughter of some city officials who said I had stolen and demolished their city gate and it was time I paid for it.

Apparently, they had more in mind for me then just laughing at me, however. I was bound and held down while my eyes were gouged out, one by one, with a hot poker. I thought I had a high tolerance level for pain. Now I was not so sure.

My new routine became sleeping a few hours and being awakened while it was still dark to mill grain. Over and over, I did the mindless work of a slave tied to a milling machine. Over and over, my mind ran back over so many things I regretted.

I remembered the first time I became involved with a woman. I knew it was not how God ordained sex. I knew it was not his plan for anyone, let alone a Nazarite. I knew he had someone in mind for me one day within the people of my faith. But I felt so alone back then, and I did not want to wait on God's time or God's ways. I wanted what Samson wanted, and I wanted it now.

Now look at me.

I never played that tape through of what this might cost me. After all, I was getting away with it, and the consequences did not catch up with me back then. I now played the tapes over and over, and the regrets and pain made those short-lived moments of pleasure seem foolish. Then my mind would turn to Delilah. Of all the regrets, that was the hardest. I thought there was something to what we had. I could not get out of my mind the picture of her taking the money—money that came from her betrayal and that put me where I was today.

The daily grind (no pun intended) left me plenty of time to recall the good moments as well. I recalled growing up with Dad and Mom teaching me about God. My dad warned me of the dangers of neglecting my faith and shared the miraculous stories of our ancestors in the faith. I was so glad that my parents were no longer alive to know what had become of their only child—their Nazarite.

I wondered how much they had heard before their deaths about how far I had strayed. I did love my mom and dad, but addiction has a way of putting what you want over what your family needs. I pushed all those voices aside back then and thought little of how it was affecting them—or anyone else, for that matter.

Some days I wondered if it was too late, if God had forgotten or abandoned me.

I recalled, however, that even in my disobedience, God had been patient and taken care of me.

In fact, it seemed that God had used me despite my failures. He had clearly fulfilled some of his purposes even when I made the wrong choices. He used me to fight for his people and rescue them from the one-sided domination and control they had been under from the Philistines. I recalled after killing one thousand of them with the jawbone, that I thanked God for empowering me and asked him to provide for my thirst, and he had.

Even during my rebellion, God protected me and had his hand on me. There is a point, however, where God allows us to reap the consequences of our own behaviors, and for me, that time had come.

Gradually, my faith was returning. In my blindness, I was seeing God more clearly than I had in my days of seeing. When I could see, I had become distracted with women, with pleasure, with all that I desired for myself. Now that I could not see, I looked beyond the physical world and saw God's plans, God's patience, God's provision.

It was the day of a great festival, celebrating Dagon, their pagan god of the Philistines. I was paraded out in front of a host of drunken idolaters who were praising their god for delivering me to them. If only they could know that it was my own free will that gave me up. Their god had no power.

My God is the only true God, the Higher Power who was restoring me to a true understanding of him and of his truth. Was it too late for God to get the glory through my life? Was it too late for me to help my people experience his deliverance through me?

As I pondered these questions, I cried out for wisdom, for strength, and for direction. I finally surrendered my life and will to his control and not my own. I offered myself and begged him to use me again. While I wished this meant being set free and living a long productive life, I was ready to give whatever it took, including my own life, to serve my God and rescue my people.

I realized I was surrounded by thousands and thousands of ungodly leaders in the pagan worship of Dagon. Perhaps it was not too late to fulfill my calling and bring deliverance to my people. My mind was spinning, not sure if it was God's will or mine, but determined to make a difference one last time.

"Young man, could you move me closer to these pillars?" I asked one of the guards. "I am getting tired from standing so long and just need to lean up against something,"

I placed one hand on each pillar, prayed, and asked God for help one last time. I asked him to help me pull down the temple and set the record straight, executing justice. Whether I lived or died, I wanted to be used by him one more time.

Still struggling between wanting revenge for myself and wanting justice and glory for God, I asked for his will to be done and began pushing with all my might. It did not come as easy as it used to. My strength was just returning, My hair had not grown out fully, and my faith was still weak.

I felt the pillars give way, and I felt the crumbling of the first one, then another. I heard cries of desperation as people fell around me. I felt little pain as I was filled with gratitude for God's mercy and peace that I would soon be safe in his hands.

No matter what you may have done and no matter how far you may have slipped down your slippery slope, do not fear. God is not finished with you until you breathe your last breath.

As long as he has spared you, he has plans for you. Call out to him today. Surrender your will and life to his care. No human power is as great as his, and no choice you make is greater than choosing to follow him. Thank you for letting me share.

Questions for Reflection:

1. How do you think a promising young man like Samson got started in this behavior?
2. Have you ever struggled with an addiction to something that was contrary to your values but that you could not stop in your power?
3. What other character defects do you see in Samson?
4. What character defects contribute to your hurtful habits or addictions?
5. When do you see Samson ignoring the warning signs? When have you failed to heed the warning signs for relapse in your life?
6. How do you feel about Samson being included in the hall of faith in Hebrews 11?
7. Does the story of Samson give you hope? If so, how?

Principles for Recovery:

1. The more you rationalize, the less you recover.
2. Doing what makes a boy happy may hinder what makes a man healthy.
3. If you don't play the tapes through before the battle, you will be playing them over and over after the defeat.
4. Who you trust will determine how you live.

Belittled but Still Believing!

(Hannah's Story)

I am a beloved wife and child of God who struggles with envy, jealousy, and low self-worth. I am the survivor of verbal and emotional abuse. My name is Hannah.

Elkanah was the love of my life. We were happy together, and he was good to me. When I was unable to have children, however, his family pressured him to take another wife in an effort to produce a family heir. Many families at the time consisted of more than one wife per husband. I had hoped we would be different. I wanted to have him just to myself.

Not having children brought a stigma and shame, and I knew I had no choice but to support him. Even my mom was telling him to do what he had to do in order to have children. Some wanted him to divorce me.

Elkanah insisted that he loved me and would never consider that to be an option. He did agree to a second wife, and Peninnah joined our family.

Peninnah had a baby almost immediately. I was so jealous. Every time the baby cooed or smiled, it was a reminder of what I did not have. I envied Peninnah. It may have been easier if she had a different attitude. She knew how much I wanted a child and appeared to relish the fact that I didn't. Soon they had a second child, then a third.

Peninnah used the fact she had children against me. She would tell him that she needed to talk to him alone about one of the children, then watch for my reaction. When my eyes welled up with tears, she would smirk and casually walk away. I tried to keep my distance and to stay in my part of the house.

The hardest time of the year was our annual trip to the tabernacle for Passover. We lived in a small town, Ramah, about fifteen miles from the tabernacle. Traveling meant a long day and night together, and I dreaded that overnight time around her.

This was an important time for families—parents would explain the meaning of Passover to their children. I sat on the sidelines watching Elkanah and Peninnah teaching their children.

Passover also meant the head of the house gave portions of meat to the wife and children. While Elkanah gave me what he could, it was hard to watch Peninnah take those extra portions for her kids. This was also a difficult time because the feast lasted for eight days—eight very long days!

I was often expected to prepare and serve meals to the others while Peninnah remained busy with her children. And Elkanah often had to help tend to the children, leaving him little time for me.

The hardest part of all was Peninnah. She wasn't just content to enjoy that extra time with Elkanah. She seemed to relish the opportunity to taunt and bully me, reminding me I had no children of my own. She would laugh whenever she sensed my sadness and would repeat to me any comments she'd heard from others about why Elkanah's "other" wife hadn't been blessed with offspring.

She was clever in not saying too much in front of Elkanah. She waited until he was out of earshot, then would laugh at me and show me how many portions she had for all of her children. She made sure I knew what the in-laws had said about how glad they were that Elkanah had married her. She spared no words in questioning to my face why God had not given me children and even suggested that I may be at fault. She told me all the theories about women not having children because of sin in their lives or because God knew they could not handle being a mother.

I did not feel like eating. I could not stop the tears from flowing. Elkanah would worry about me and ask me what was wrong. I tried not to worry him. When I did tell him what Peninnah said, it was hard for him to believe because she was so good at hiding this behavior from him. When he confronted her, she played innocent and said I must have misunderstood. When I told him how hard it was not having children, he minimized my concerns.

Men just don't understand.

Elkanah meant well, but he didn't help anything when he suggested I was being too sensitive and that it shouldn't bother me so much to not have children. How would he know? He had children. And the pressure that society placed was upon the woman and not the man. How could he say I was being too sensitive?

He was just trying to help when he asked if having him was not "better to me than having ten sons?" (1 Samuel 1:8)

But the answer was a definite "no, it is not!"

Don't get me wrong, he was a good husband, and he tried to console me. Sometimes, though, you just need someone to listen and not try to fix things. He wanted to fix more than to listen. I wanted to be heard more than to be helped. And no matter how much he loved me, I had trouble internalizing any words of encouragement because I felt like a failure. Because of my own beliefs about myself, it was easier to believe what Peninnah said than what he did.

One year, it was more than I could handle. Don't ask me why all these years I had not thought of this, but I decided to let God know of my anguish. Perhaps I had avoided telling God my true feelings because of my sense of worthlessness. Perhaps I was fearful that maybe it was true that he had cursed me for something wrong in my life. I was unsure of how God looked at me. I was sure of one thing, however; he was the only one who could change my situation.

I got up from one of those long feasts, which I was not eating anyway, and headed to the tabernacle. I don't remember all that

I said, but through my tears, I told God my dreams for being a mother. I told him how hard it was not being able to have children. I told him about the verbal abuse that I went through every year.

Telling God all that I felt, I also promised him something. As much as I wanted to raise a son, should he bless me with one, I committed that I would bring that son back here to live at the tabernacle to assist Eli the priest. Eli was getting old, and I was sure he could use the help; and if God would answer this impossible request, I wanted him to know that I would show my appreciation with giving my son back.

I did not know if God would hear me. My view of God was distorted by my experiences with people. I always seemed to base my value on something out of my control, the ability to have children.

The most damaging thing about verbal abuse is not what is said to us but what it does to us. Whether he answered or not, I knew I had prayed my heart out, and I was done.

Eli started walking over to me with a troubled look on his face. He was close enough to see that my lips were moving but not close enough to hear the words that I whispered in my prayers. To him, I appeared like a woman who had been intoxicated. He feared that I had been feasting for the wrong reasons, and he began scolding me for coming here drunk! I quickly set the record straight, hoping that he would believe me.

To my surprise, he did. Instead of brushing it off with a half-hearted apology, he proceeded to bless me and told me, "Go in peace! May the God of Israel grant your request!" (1 Samuel 1:17)

I walked away feeling as if a fifty-pound weight had been removed from my shoulders. Talking to God and having this reassurance from Eli, I felt hope again. My faith was rekindled. I no longer was worried about what anyone else had to say about me. I had given my burden to God, and now I was trusting Him to do His will. I could eat again, and my tears had subsided. Elkanah could tell things were different, and I told him about my prayer and my encounter with Eli. We laughed about my almost getting kicked out of the tabernacle for appearing drunk!

It wasn't long until it happened. I was pregnant. I was going to be a mother. Nobody could now accuse me of being cursed by God or of being less of a woman. As I thanked God for this gift of life within me, I realized that I had given Peninnah too much power over me.

I also began to feel compassion for her. While I had always wondered why she was so hateful and spiteful, I began to realize something. She was jealous of me! While I envied her ability to have children, she envied my relationship with Elkanah. As much as she loved having children, she always knew that I was his favorite and his first love. This was hard for her. They say that hurt people often hurt people. Indeed, Peninnah's own hurt caused her to hurt me for many years. Sometimes people who appear the most confident can be the most insecure. With God's help, I began to forgive her and pray for her.

The big day finally arrived. I soon forgot the uncomfortable back pain, the nausea of morning sickness, and the pain of childbirth. It was a boy! We named him Samuel. I gave God all the glory and thanked him for this gift. I also did not forget my promise to him regarding my son. I tried not to think too far ahead about how hard it would be to leave him at the tabernacle when the time came, and I focused on the joy of having him resting in my arms and drinking from my breasts.

While I now know that whether you have a baby or not does not change your value to God, I felt relieved to know that I was not "too bad" to be a mother, and that Peninnah's words were not true that God could not trust me with one of his children.

When the time for the yearly feast came, it was still too early to leave Samuel. I could have taken him with me and gone. In fact, my old insecure and jealous self would have made sure I went, just to keep an eye on Elkanah and Peninnah.

He told me I could come. "No," I assured him, "I will wait until it's time to leave him there and will stay home this year."

It crossed my mind that it would be a chance to rub it in Peninnah's face that I was now a mom as well and that she had been wrong about me. I was learning, however, to let things go and let God handle them. Holding onto bitterness would only keep me in bondage to what I held it for. No, I would stay home and focus on my blessings and enjoy my son while I had him.

The time came all too soon. Some wondered if I would follow through. I know that sometimes people make bargains with God and then go back on them. I had meant every word, however. God was the source of this gift, and I intended to give him back to God. Don't misunderstand me, it was the most difficult day of my life. Difficult and yet full of God's grace and peace. Painful but full of the assurance that I was doing the right thing.

As I took Samuel to meet the aging priest, Eli, I reminded him of our conversation years earlier. He chuckled as I reminded him that he thought I was drunk! I reiterated my intentions of having Samuel serve and assist him in any way needed. It was comforting to see the joy on his face in being able to have a young child come and offer company and assistance.

As we all learned in the following years, his sons were not following the Lord too well, and it broke his heart. Having Samuel there was like a second chance to him. He could pass on so much wisdom and guidance to our son.

As heavy as our hearts were, we took time to worship. Worship is not just for the happy times, like when Samuel was born. It is also for the hard times, when saying goodbye. Worship is for God because he deserves it at all times. Worship is also for us, as it helps us stay focused and to keep all of life in perspective.

I worshipped the Lord with praise for answered prayer, for being holy, for being our rock, and for providing our needs, and most of all I praised him for his merciful heart.

"He lifts the poor from the dust and the needy from the garbage dump!" (1 Samuel 2:8) That phrase would later end up in one of the Psalms (113:7).

Who would have thought that God would use my simple words to encourage so many others?

Leaving was hard. There were a lot of tears as we started down the road back to Ramah. Yet I knew that this was where Samuel needed to be. This was the right thing to do. I knew that God had big plans for Samuel. A mother knows these things.

Thankfully, we returned every year and were able to see how Samuel was doing. Leaving was still hard but became easier year by year, especially as we saw him thriving there. I took him a new coat each year. I began stitching the next one almost as soon as delivering the last.

With each stitch, I thought about my Samuel and how he was doing. With each thought, I prayed that God was keeping his hand on him and that Eli had wisdom and strength, even at his age, to raise our son. Eli seemed to look forward to our visits too. He always took time to pray for us and thank God for our son. He also prayed that God would bless us with other children to take the place of the son we had allowed him to raise. God answered those prayers, and I was blessed with three more sons and two beautiful daughters.

Rumors had spread that Eli's sons were abusing their power and taking advantage of others. They finally had to be removed from leadership. At times, I worried about Samuel growing up with Eli. Had Eli's failures in parenting created the problems with his boys? If so, would Samuel suffer from poor parenting as well? Over time, those worries proved unfounded, however, and it was clear that God had used Eli in Samuel's life to grow up as a man of God.

One visit, Eli told us how God had spoken directly to Samuel and had used Samuel to present an important message to him. I never asked what the message was. It didn't seem like my place.

We were proud to see God using Samuel as he was growing up. Eli was relying on him more and more, and Samuel was becoming an important leader respected by all.

Soon it was clear that young Samuel had found his calling as a prophet. I no longer had to wait until visits to Shiloh to hear news of Samuel. He was now considered a prophet and leader, filling a much needed gap in our nation's history. People spoke of him everywhere.

Things seemed better with Peninnah. This was not necessarily because she treated me better, but I had learned to take her words less seriously. I was learning emotional boundaries. Just because she said something did not make it true. Just because she believed it did not mean that I had to believe it.

While her insecurities and jealousy were probably greater now that I had as many children as she did, I no longer reacted the way I had in the past. I did not let her words get to me. I did not stop eating. I did not cry uncontrollably. It still hurt, but I let things go sooner. I stayed focused on raising my children. I worried less what Peninnah thought. I started listening more to my husband's positive voice than to her negative one. Soon, I was also having more positive thoughts myself.

Another key for me was learning to live for more than my own happiness. Having children allowed me to spend more time thinking of others and less about myself. As I prayed for my children and bandaged their injuries, I thought less about my own desires.

As I focused on helping them grow up well, I concerned myself less with what anyone else said about me. Sometimes Peninnah or her kids would pick on my children, and this was hard to watch. I focused, however, on helping them see their own value, and I was determined to teach them to see themselves how God saw them and not how others treated them.

As hurtful as Peninnah's abusive words were in my life, I am thankful that the pain I felt in the midst of her words is what drove me to a deeper life of prayer to my Heavenly Father. I learned that he cares about everything that I go through. He heard my prayers and gave me other relationships to focus upon.

No matter what you are going through, bring that pain to him. Let him know your need and requests. Then surrender it all to him!

If you have someone in your life who is verbally or emotionally abusive, I hope my story encourages you in knowing that you are not alone. I know what it feels like to be the target of someone else's hurtful words and degrading comments. I know how much harder it is when that person lives in the same house, when you can't get away. I know how difficult it is not to take to heart the hurtful words. Sometimes that person's voice becomes the only one you can hear.

I do hope that you will listen for other voices, ones that encourage you and build you up instead of tear you down. Choose to surround yourself with those voices as much as possible until those voices become the one within you.

Do not define yourself by how people see you or by what they might have said but by the God who created you and loves you. Thank you for letting me share.

Questions for Reflection:

1. Can you relate to being the target of someone else's verbal abuse?
2. Why did Peninnah continue to berate Hannah, and how did this affect her?
3. How do we give power to the negative voices around us and often ignore the positive messages instead?
4. Do you think Peninnah stopped being jealous of Hannah? Why or why not?
5. How did Elkanah try to encourage Hannah? Why did that not work out?

6. Have you ever had a day that was both difficult and wonderful at the same time?

Principles for Recovery:

1. Sometimes it is more important to be heard than to be helped.
2. Don't define yourself by the words of an abuser but by the love of your Creator.
3. When you cannot change the facts, you can still change your focus.
4. When you accept hardship as a pathway to peace, you will experience healing and a life full of purpose.

When a Godly King Hits Bottom

(David's Story)

I grew up as the youngest of eight boys, somewhat over-looked and relegated to the position of delivery boy. When my brothers went to war, I tended sheep. I was blessed with godly parents who were respected in the community, and I had a great friend named Jonathan. I was even called a man after God's own heart. Nevertheless, I struggled with sexual immorality and selfish decisions. My name is David.

Bethlehem, my hometown, wasn't large, but it was only five miles from the capital, so we stayed connected to all that was happening in the big city. My primary responsibility in the family was caring for our sheep, so I spent much of my time in the beautiful countryside of rolling hills and fertile pastures.

It sometimes felt like I was only out watching sheep because I was not considered old enough for the more important tasks, like going to war. I enjoyed those moments of solitude, however, and taught myself to play a harp and got to be pretty good at it. I composed much of my own music, with the lyrics coming directly from the journals I kept of my thoughts and prayers.

I did not doubt my ability to protect myself or my sheep. Like other shepherds, I utilized a slingshot to protect our flock. My heart stopped that time I saw a bear going after one of the lambs. It was already too close, and there wasn't time to wind up a slingshot. I grabbed my other weapon, a large club that I kept nearby, just in case. I hit him quick and hard, in time for him to release the lamb from his jaws. On another occasion, I took out a lion. While they say slingshots are not as accurate, I prayed hard and practiced often and became confident in using this weapon whenever needed. Soon I would use it to protect more than just my little flock.

I often had to deliver lunch to my oldest three brothers. On one particular day, while they were fighting in the war against the Philistines, I came as usual, with their food. The Philistines had a new warrior, a giant named Goliath, who was intimidating our soldiers and striking terror in our king. I found myself watching him too, that day, as he stood on the hill and called out at our men to come and fight. While he was quite frightening and striking, the thing that amazed me most was the fact that NONE of our brave soldiers made a sound in response to his challenges and curses.

Eliab, my oldest brother, was not too happy when he saw me and heard that I was questioning why no one had stepped up to fight the giant. "What are you doing around here anyway? Where have you left those few sheep that you are supposed to be taking care of? You just want to see the battle." (1 Samuel 17:28)

His belittling accusations stung, especially when he questioned my motives, then called me prideful and deceitful. It is hard to be falsely accused. It was not the first time that Eliab got on me.

"What have I done this time?" I asked. "I was only asking a question!"

I wondered, as I walked away, if Eliab was jealous after Samuel had anointed me to be the future king. When Samuel showed up at our house, it was everyone's assumption that Eliab was the logical choice. He was the oldest. He was tall and strong. It was a shock to all of them, beginning with Eliab, when God told Samuel that he was not the one. One by one, Samuel met each of my brothers, and one by one, he proceeded to tell Dad that each was not the one chosen.

Finally, and only because Samuel was so insistent, they called for me. It was then that I, the youngest and least experienced in war or leadership of any kind, was chosen. Is this why Eliab seemed to be so hard on me? Is this why he always minimized my job with the sheep?

My thoughts jolted back to the present challenge. If nobody else was stepping up, maybe I should. Next thing I knew, the king had summoned me. Apparently he heard me asking about this Goliath and was concerned that I may be thinking about taking him on. King Saul had been good to me so far. When dealing with some emotional and spiritual issues that put him in a downcast state of mind, his attendants would summon me to come play the harp. It always seemed to cheer him up and set his mind back on track.

The king, however, was not too thrilled about my offer to go fight Goliath.

"Don't be ridiculous!" he began. "There's no way you can fight this Philistine and possibly win. You're only a boy, and he's been a man of war from his youth!" (1 Samuel 17:33)

It was not exactly a vote of confidence. Not one to give up, I persisted until he knew it was no use. I was ready to fight this giant to the death, and I knew that God was on our side.

"At least take my armor," Saul insisted. You should have seen me swimming in the king's armor! It was heavy, large, and extremely awkward, to say the least. If I was to fight, I needed to fight as who I was and not as someone else. I gathered my slingshot and picked up five stones on the way to meet this pagan antagonist who dared to challenge the people of God.

His roaring laughter echoed across the valley. Goliath seemed to be both amused and annoyed that someone of my age was coming out to accept his challenge. He cursed me in the names of his gods. This motivated me all the more. This was not just my reputation at stake. I was here to represent our God and prove his power, not mine.

I looked at this giant. I could tell everyone was aware of just how small we all were in comparison to Goliath. I chose, however, to see his size in comparison to that of God. In that light, he looked very small.

"You come to me with sword, spear, and javelin, but I come to you in the name of the Lord whom you have defied!" I responded. (1 Samuel 17:45) God gave me the faith at that moment to face the incredible odds that I was up against and not to back down. As I let that first stone rip, it went straight for the one spot on his forehead that was not covered by his huge helmet. He fell to the ground with a tremendous thud.

That day marked the beginning of many things. I was no longer just a boy watching sheep but a man ready to fight the enemy. I also earned the respect of the people of Israel, despite the fact that they were not privy to the fact that I had been anointed to serve as the next king. This respect came at a cost to my relationship with King Saul, however. I wish those ladies had not started that song and dance about Saul killing thousands but me killing ten thousands! That really set him off.

Saul began to see me as a threat to his power. He was jealous of me and afraid that I would take his kingdom. His fear and jealousy fed his anger issues. On more than one occasion, he even got so angry he threw a spear to try and pin me against a wall. Thankfully, I saw it coming and got away each time. Saul was becoming emotionally unstable.

While one day Jonathan would talk him down, the next day, Saul was ready to attack me with a spear again.

Saul was determined to have control. One way he tried to control me was through letting me marry his daughter. When she realized he wanted me dead, she helped me escape. As both his son and his daughter proved to be more loyal to me than to him, Saul became furious and out of control. I was a wanted man. It hurt knowing that the man I had served faithfully both as a musician and soldier was out to take my life!

Leaving town was not easy. The king's son, Jonathan, had become my best friend. We shared everything. We loved each other with a genuine love and were closer than brothers. He always had my back. He knew that I had been appointed by God to be the next king. Despite what this meant for him, he was not jealous and supported me one hundred percent. I am sure his dad sensed this, and it only added to his dad's insecurity. My heart went out to Jonathan. It was hard to live in the home of an emotionally unstable individual. It was like walking on eggshells for him.

The next few years were both hard and yet some of the best years of my life. Living in caves and out on the run, I learned who my true friends were. My brothers and other family members came to support me. Even Eliab seemed to get over his jealousy and was there for me. Others learned of my fallout with Saul. Some of them also had issues that put them on the outs with the king. Some owed debts. Others were in trouble or just couldn't get along in society. They came to join me.

We soon had a band of four hundred misfits supporting one another in life and in battle. We knew that we all were dealing with something. We laughed when people talked about us as "those people." It was OK. We had each other. We understood what it meant to not fit in, to struggle, but also to choose to live in a supportive community. We may have been hiding from society, but we did not hide our issues from each other. We were close.

Saul's insecurities worsened, and one time he even had eighty-five priests killed just because I had been seen talking to one of them. I felt awful. My friends reminded me that it wasn't my fault, but still, it was hard to believe.

Saul began to personally lead the troops into the wilderness and caves trying to find me. A couple of times we could have killed him as we came upon him sleeping in a cave. My men were ready to do so. I told them it would be wrong—regardless of what someone has done to us, the role of vengeance is strictly for God and not us. I wanted God to determine when and how I became king, not me. Through the dangers and difficulties I faced on the run, I learned to submit to God and to trust his will and his timing. Hardship was my pathway to peace.

God's timing did come, as it always does. One day, both Saul and Jonathan died in battle. I found no solace in knowing that the man who was trying to kill me was dead. I knew Saul had issues. I chose to live in a state of forgiveness and not bitterness. I grieved his passing.

Even more, I grieved the passing of my best friend. It did not matter that we had few opportunities in those latter years to get together. Our hearts were as one. Life would not be the same without Jonathan.

I was king in Judah, but one of Saul's remaining sons sought to continue his dynasty in Israel, and for several years there was a battle raging within our divided nation. I waited on God's timing, however, and did not seek to retaliate against those who supported the other side. When one of their leaders died, I led the funeral procession to honor him. When a couple of men killed Saul's remaining son, I had them put to death. As I told all my men, God always took care of my enemies, and I did not go after individuals, regardless of what they had done to me. People saw that I was not part of the attempts for revenge and soon followed my lead in the reconciliation of our great nation.

While we were blessed with peace, I became complacent and soon lost focus. When war broke out again, I did not take my usual place, leading the charge, but decided to stay home and indulge in some time for myself. Over time, I had allowed myself to take multiple wives and many concubines. I had started missing more battles. I had become used to indulging myself within certain limits that I deemed appropriate. I enjoyed my God-given passions but soon was moving beyond my God-ordained boundaries for them. When I saw Bathsheba, I slipped to a new low.

I was not on guard, was alone, and had removed myself from accountability when I was up on the roof strolling. I had put the harp aside, stopped journaling, and was just walking around when I saw her. A beautiful woman was bathing on her roof, alone. I allowed my eyes to feast on beauty that was not intended for me and for my mind to imagine what it would be like to be with her. Soon I was making plans to send over one of my men to summon her to my palace. Nobody refused the king. I enjoyed whatever I chose and indulged however I wanted. After all, I was the king! Unfortunately, my position further isolated me from accountability by the fact that no one would question me and that everyone followed my orders.

Whether she was also lonely and wanting to have this affair, or whether she felt obligated to accept the invitation of a king, Bathsheba was certainly the vulnerable one in our relationship. I have since made amends to her for all that I did to disrupt her life, but at that moment, all I was wanting was to indulge in some self-gratifying pleasures with a beautiful woman whose husband was out of town. Yes, I knew she was married. I knew her husband. He was one of my loyal soldiers. That did not stop me. I told myself this was to be a one-time affair and that he would never find out. Nobody would.

I pushed this out of my mind. I imagined that I would never hear from Bathsheba again. We had agreed this would be our life-long secret that we would carry to the grave. When a message arrived from her one day, I imagined she was thinking about me or wanting to say how much she enjoyed our time together. I was not prepared for what was in that note.

"I am pregnant!" Three little words that changed my life. God has a way of exposing our secrets, especially the ones that violate the integrity of our relationship with him. My head was spinning with damage control. I had to make Uriah think this was his child. I had to fix the problem I had created. He was out fighting the enemy in battle, however, and had not been with his wife in a while. In that moment, I devised a plan to cover up my sin my own way—and not to deal with it God's way.

At my instruction, Uriah came to the palace, called back from battle, thinking he was there to bring a front-line report to the king. I thanked him for the report and urged him to go home and relax, spend some time with his wife. I went to bed believing that he would sleep with his wife and that all would be well when he thought she was having his baby.

Surprisingly, I found out the next morning that Uriah did not go home. "How could I go enjoy time with my wife and sleep in my own bed when my fellow soldiers are out sacrificing themselves on the battlefield?" he explained. He was ready to return and join the fight.

A tinge of guilt welled up within as I thought of what I had done with his wife while he so selflessly avoided indulging in his own God-given rights out of respect for his men. The guilt was overruled by fear—that I was going to be exposed in less than nine months.

That fear caused me to make an even greater mistake. I sent a letter to Joab, my general, from Uriah himself, to have him placed at the front lines. I then ordered for them to withdraw and ensure that he would be killed by the enemy. Once again, I relied on knowing that Joab would follow my instructions with no questions asked. I had no accountability and ran my thoughts by no one. I was as sick as my secrets.

Upon learning of his death, I brought Bathsheba to the palace. People would think that I was doing a favor to a poor widow of one of my military men by marrying her. Perhaps my secret was safe. While I felt I had dodged a bullet, my soul was not at rest. I was haunted by thoughts of what I had done. I no longer felt that closeness with God. Yet I filled my time with busyness and avoided thinking about it as much as possible.

The guilt within me chose to focus on wrongdoing around me to avoid facing my own sin. I had lost my usual forgiving nature and was quick to snap, quick to judge, and quick to condemn others. When Nathan the prophet told me a scenario of a man who had done far less than me and asked what should be done to him, I exploded in anger at this selfish individual he was telling me about! Yet right below the surface of my shallow layer of anger was a heart full of regrets and guilt over my own selfishness—a heart ready to explode from shame.

Then Nathan dared to put his finger in my face and brought some accountability and truth back into my life. My secret was exposed. My denial was shattered. I stood there weeping and confessed all that I had done. Then my accuser became my comforter, as men of God who hold us accountable are meant to be. He assured me that despite the consequences on the horizon and the impending loss of my child, God had already seen my repentant heart, and I was forgiven!

I grieved over the loss of our child. I wept over the sins I now chose to face fully and honestly. I journaled many of my feelings as I took inventory of what I had done. Despite all the individuals who had been hurt by my actions, my greatest sin was not against Uriah, Bathsheba, my other wives, or the other soldiers who lost a comrade in battle. My greatest sin was against God. I had taken life that he had created. I had violated laws he had put in place. "Against you only have I sinned," I wrote. (Psalm 51:4)

"Forgive me for shedding blood!" I cried. And then I worshipped. It had been a long time since I worshipped so freely and truthfully. God responded, not to some huge sacrifice, but to a broken and contrite spirit that humbly begged for his mercy.

As I humbled myself, I began to see how my decisions had caused so much dysfunction in my family.

Through neglecting God's intentions of one woman for one man, I had acquired multiple wives. My children had issues of jealousy, of rebellion, and even of the sexual sins of rape, incest, and murder. In my focus on my job as king, and of my times of self-centered obsessions, whether it was chasing Bathsheba or other women to join my harem, I neglected my wives and children and was passive in offering leadership at home. One of my sons, Absalom, even tried to take the kingdom from me. In the process, he slept with my concubines and betrayed me through deception and lies.

When Absalom was killed, I mourned. I had many regrets. Even though he was my enemy, he was foremost my son. I was stuck in my regrets and grief. Joab had to confront me to let this go because my public mourning was putting a damper on the morale of our nation, and he reminded me the kingdom had just been saved! Thankfully, I had learned to put accountability in my life, and I took his words to heart. I am thankful for this man becoming one of my accountability partners.

It is humbling to know that I have been called a "man after God's own heart." I take no pride in what good others may say about me, however, because I know the mistakes I have made and the lives I have damaged. If there is any truth to me being a man after God's own heart, it must relate to my heart of forgiveness and desire for reconciliation. Despite the hurts I experienced from Saul, from my son Absalom, and from others who sided with him, I have chosen the road to forgiveness. God is the only judge of our hearts, and he has forgiven me so much. How can I withhold that same forgiveness from others?

I hope that with God's help, you will also look at your life, let go of those secret sins that need to be released, live in accountability, and choose the road to forgiveness. It is the only way any of us can be people after God's own heart! Be broken, be real, and don't be afraid to be one of those people! Thank you for letting me share.

Questions for Reflection:

1. David's sins were compounded by his isolation and lack of accountability. When have you been vulnerable due to isolation from others?

2. David was very conscious of God's forgiveness and also appeared to do well in forgiving others. How are you doing in the area of forgiveness?

3. David's children had some severe dysfunction. What did you hear in his story about this? What types of dysfunction have you had to deal with in your family?

4. Why do you think that David was so angry in his reaction when Nathan presented him with the story of a seemingly lesser sin while he was hiding his own?

5. David had a band of followers when hiding in the caves who all seemed to relate to being outsiders on the run. Have you ever been part of this type of community?

Principles for Recovery:

1. When you are motivated by a greater purpose, you will be guided by a greater power.

2. Complacency leads to indulgence; indulgence leads to relapse.

3. When you stop fighting together, you start losing alone.

4. People who don't deal with their own failures tend to be consumed with the failures of others.

Depressed but Not Done!

(Elijah's Story)

Have you ever felt ready to throw in the towel? Maybe felt useless? That all your efforts were in vain, and why bother anymore? I know how you feel.

I am a firm follower of Jehovah who struggles with depression. My name is Elijah.

You may have heard of me—the miracles, the fire called down from heaven, the courageous prophet of God who dared to face the prophets of Baal. There's more to the story, though.

Nobody would have accused me of lacking in faith, and no one suspected that I struggled with doubts. I was the poster child for faith. When God told me to move, I moved. When God told me to speak, I spoke.

Many times I only knew the next step. I went where God told me to go, and he provided everything I needed along the way.

Once he told me to camp by a brook, and I did. Ravens showed up with food, just as I became hungry. I called it "meals on wings."

The nation's famine grew worse, and when the meals stopped coming, I wasn't sure what would happen next. God told me to visit a widow—not exactly where I would expect a great supply of food. I followed and God provided. My faith was strengthened, and hers was established, while God kept her supply coming. Later, he used me to restore her son's life.

I faced Jezebel and Ahab, other kings and queens, and nobles and princes. I did not cut corners. I told it like it was. I predicted famine and prophesied deliverance. I had struggles but always stuck it out and saw the victories. There were challenges, but God always saw me through.

I didn't expect that I would be dealing with depression, but it hit right after my most important victory. In fact, I don't know about you, but a lot of my bouts with depression, or feeling blue, seemed to happen right after things were going pretty well.

I had been up on Mt. Carmel and had challenged the prophets of Baal to pray to their idol and call down fire to consume their offering. It was quite comical, actually, watching them dance around pleading with a god who did not exist to answer prayers that were getting nowhere! I admit, I poked a little fun at them. I suggested maybe they needed to cry out louder because maybe their god was asleep, maybe away on a trip. I even suggested he might be busy going to the bathroom. I guess I got carried away in the moment.

I was really sad to see them go so far as to cut themselves to somehow get the attention or win the affection of their so-called "god." I'm so glad I don't have to torture myself to get my God's attention.

Nothing happened despite all their efforts. Then I called everyone over to see what the real God could do. No cutting myself, no screaming at the top of my lungs. In fact I even had them pour water on the altar several times to make it more challenging and more amazing when God sent the fire that I knew he would send.

And send the fire he did! Wow, what an amazing day—fire blazing down from heaven, consuming everything in its path: the sacrifice, the wood, even the stones! People started crying out, "The Lord is God! The Lord is God!"

What a day!

That was literally my mountaintop experience. I just knew this was the beginning of something big and that finally an army of believers was rising up! I was on top of the world spiritually and emotionally as I headed down from the mountain that day.

I wish I could have just kept that feeling. I wish I could have just kept believing how wonderful God is. I wish I could have kept that courage and that energy going! I should have prayed harder. I should have remembered all my blessings. If only I had not isolated myself so soon! If only I had—oh, never mind. The "if onlys," the "should haves," and the regrets just seemed to make it worse. They always do.

All it took to send me in a downward spiral was Jezebel—one annoying, deceptive, hurtful woman. I let her get the best of me. Once I knew she was out for my life, all the miracles and all the answered prayer in the world was not enough. I ran.

I should have known better. I had faced her before, and God had pulled me through. But I seemed to forget.

Not only did I run, but I left my faithful servant and only true human companion behind. I failed to think about him or how he felt. All I knew was that I wanted to be alone. I did not want to see anybody or talk to anybody. I just wanted to seclude myself. I got as far away from everyone as possible. I went into the desert and sat under a tree all by myself.

Poor me! I was alone, devastated, and losing hope. I felt awful!

I was even shutting God out until I realized I needed to talk to him. When I did, my prayer was not a prayer of faith by any means.

My prayer went something like this: "Dear God, I have had enough. Just take my life and let me die. I feel worthless." It all seemed meaningless and useless now. God did not need me. He hardly seemed to care even after all I had done for him. I did not deserve to feel this way.

I began to doubt it all—*maybe I am worthless. Perhaps God and everyone else would be better off without me.* Yes, that is how I felt. Then I lay down and slept under that old tree. I slept and slept and slept. That is all I felt like doing. Anything to escape the awful pain and ache of being alive. Anything to keep from feeling what I felt when I was awake.

Then something strange happened. I woke up and someone was touching me, gently nudging me to eat some freshly baked bread and drink some water. It shocked me but also got my attention. Why did God send someone to do this for me? I thought for sure that God would be angry at me for feeling the way I felt. *Doesn't God get angry when I feel negative things about him? Shouldn't I just have more faith and get over it and act like everything is fine?*

The gesture was helpful, but I didn't necessarily feel all better. Depression doesn't go away that easily. I really didn't want to feel this anymore, but I felt powerless to feel any other way.

As soon as I ate, I lay down again and went back to sleep. I have no idea how long I slept. It all seemed like a blur, really.

Then there was that person, that angel, tapping on my shoulder again—trying to get me to eat. I really did not have much of an appetite. It was a chore to eat. It took everything in me just to sit up. I did not feel like doing anything anymore. But something about his persistence gave me a feeling that maybe here is someone who cares what happens to me—it made me listen. It stirred some hope within me.

As I listened, this messenger of God told me that I had a long journey ahead. I needed to eat again and prepare myself. I was still expecting some kind of rebuke for my sleeping, my not eating, leaving my servant behind, my fear and lack of faith. But there was nothing but a gentle voice encouraging me to eat.

I have to admit, the idea of a journey was not very comforting! I did not want to leave that tree—that was my place of comfort. I did not want to move an inch! Surely nothing good could come from leaving or moving. It felt risky. And think of all the energy that would require. *Oh well, I guess I could at least eat and think about it later.* I can't say I was excited about the trip; in fact, I was not even sure where I was supposed to go! Maybe I was just supposed to get moving again? I finally got the energy together to begin. This was not easy. It was like having to pick up my foot with both hands just to take that first step! I ended up going to Mt. Sinai. Maybe if I went to the place were God had spoken to Moses, I could find him again. Each day felt like forever. In fact, most people made this trip in fourteen days—it took me forty. That's right, it took forty days because I was so down and had such little energy that those same things that usually seemed to be easy felt impossible.

I dreaded each morning. I would wake up in the middle of the night and hope that it was not time to get up. Then there were other days that I could not get to sleep, and I dreaded night and wanted it to be morning. I was a mess! *Why had I even started this journey? Would I find God again? Did he care? Did anyone?*

I finally made it and found a cave. Guess what I did first there? I slept. I thought maybe I would spend the rest of my life in that cave—away from everyone and all the difficulties of life. Maybe I could forget about my failures and about all the people who had abandoned me or were out to hurt me.

Suddenly I heard a voice. I thought for a minute I was delusional or having a psychotic experience related to being depressed. There was something different about that voice. The moment I heard it, I knew this was God, and it was not an illusion.

I was still a little afraid, though, that maybe now God was ready to punish me for being fearful and depressed or for not serving him better. Yet I came to realize that it was also God who had sent the food and given me the strength to take this trip, so maybe I should give him a chance! I listened. It was not a rebuke, but it was a question. "What am I doing here, you ask?" It seemed like God already knew the answer to that. All I could imagine was that he was asking for my benefit. Still, I found myself angry to even be asked. *I'll tell him what I'm doing there.*

"I've been serving you with everything I have, God. These people have torn down your altars and killed all your prophets. I'm the only one left," I said. "Now they are trying to kill me. That's what I am doing here."

God seemed to know that I could not have handled him coming on too strong. Thinking back, I am sure he probably felt like shaking me up a bit. At least that is how I tended to react when other people were not responding to my help or advice. But God just told me to get out of the cave and wait on the mountain. That seemed kind of risky, but I had come this far. So, I pulled myself up. I stepped out and walked over to the side of the mountain. Recovery also involves risk. What did I have to lose? I went.

I stood there and waited. I heard a windstorm hit the mountain. Was God going to bring me a revelation or a warning through this storm? No. Nothing.

Then an earthquake hit the mountain. I stood there trembling. God was up to something.

Then I saw a fire, reminding me of that fire on that other mountain. That seemed such a long time ago now. Maybe God was going to give me that same feeling I had on that other mountain again. But still nothing.

Then a whisper. It was God's voice again. Quiet and gentle. Loving. Wait, he was asking me the same question again. Talk about patience—and love. He could have written me off by now, but he did not. I felt kind of funny giving him the same answer.

There is something about being depressed. You just get stuck on the same ideas, the same thoughts, living in the same ruts—the same thing over and over. So, I told him again why I was at this place and in this state of mind.

Now maybe God would leave me alone. *If he is not going to judge me for lacking faith or for being depressed, maybe he would at least leave me alone and realize I am no good to him anymore.* That is what I wanted anyway, wasn't it? To be left alone. To have no more demands placed on me. At least if I don't try, I won't feel like the failure that I know I am.

But God kept talking. It sounded like he had not written me off. Instead, he was giving me instructions for another assignment. Actually, he was rattling off more than one assignment. Go through Damascus and anoint a new king in Syria. That sounded a lot better than going back to Israel.

Oh, also anoint a new king in Israel after that. Then start discipling a guy named Elisha who will become a prophet. I could not believe my ears. God was not finished with me and I could still make a difference in this world. Even when I was ready to exclude God from my plans, he wanted to include me in his!

I thought I was the only prophet left in Israel, but I was definitely mistaken. In fact, God said there were seven thousand still left. I was only off by 6,999! That's what my depression had done to me. Because I felt alone, I believed I was alone. Because I felt useless, I believed I was useless.

Even though I began to believe God didn't care for me, he still very much did. He loved me and was not about to leave me. I had pulled away from him, but he had never left me. He had not abandoned me. Even when I ended up stuck in a cave, he was there with me—patiently waiting for me to realize it. He wanted me to step outside the cave so he could feed me again and give me perspective.

Even when the trip takes forty days, one that takes others fourteen, it's OK. God will give me strength for the journey and provide all that I need. He will even provide companions and encouragement along the way. But it is up to me to invite those companions in and not leave them behind.

That's my story. I don't know what you're going through today—if you are feeling lost or alone, as I did. But I know this—God loves you more than you will ever be able to figure out. He wants to bring purpose into your life. That purpose will probably mean moving out of your comfort zone, building new relationships, and letting him bring some new perspective. He will probably ask you some questions and challenge your thinking along the way, but don't be afraid.

God will be gentle with you. He knows what you need and will send help for you to get past anything in your path. I know he did for me. God bless you, and thanks for letting me share.

Questions for Reflection:

1. Do you relate to any of Elijah's symptoms of depression in his story?
2. When have you felt discouraged or depressed after a time of victory?
3. Elijah thought he was the only one left when there were really seven thousand who still followed God. How does depression distort our thinking?
4. How did God give Elijah a new purpose to help get him back on track?
5. Why do you think God spoke to Elijah in a still small voice and not in the thunder or in the earthquake?
6. What strategies do you see God implementing in helping Elijah get out of his depression?

Principles for Recovery:

1. You cannot change the onset of depression, but you can avoid an outcome of despair.
2. Physical care is essential to emotional regulation.
3. You won't rise to the future if you are stuck in the past.
4. Depression distorts your thinking, clouds your perspective, and overshadows your dreams.
5. To regain purpose for your life, you need to reconnect with the one who gave it to you.

A Proud General Gets Dunked!

(Naaman's Story)

I thought I had it all. I was a well-respected general in the Syrian army. I lived in a nice house with a beautiful wife and had plenty of help! I was a proud man, in good health, and feared nothing until one day I came down with a dreaded, terminal disease called leprosy. Today I am a grateful believer and recipient of God's healing. I struggle with pride, anger, and stubbornness, and my name is Naaman.

I was proud of what I had. After all, I had earned it. I had the king's respect and was as close as anyone can expect to be to a king. My country had an on-again, off-again history of conflicts with Israel. During one of those conflicts, when their king had disguised himself during battle, I was the one whose bravery and skill delivered an arrow right between the armor of King Ahab. It proved to be a historic victory for my people. I would later learn that I was simply being used by God to implement discipline upon the nation of Israel and an ungodly king who needed it. God gave us that victory. At that time, however, it was all about me and my ego.

My house was filled with tokens of conquest and trophies of battle that I attributed to no one but myself.

Of all the trophies of battle, the one my wife appreciated the most was the Hebrew girl whom I found hanging back in one of the homes we had raided. While a little young, I knew we could train her and brought her home to serve my wife. She helped with chores, learned to cook the meals, and even helped my wife getting dressed each morning.

While tasks that most women could handle for themselves, the wife of a man of my status was not expected to be responsible for such matters. Over time, and due to my frequent absences, she and my wife became close. My wife respected her and the genuine faith that this young lady had in the God she still believed in, despite now living in a foreign land with foreign gods.

One day my wife noticed a skin condition developing on my hands. A few spots were feeling numb. A couple of boils on my feet made it uncomfortable to walk. Soon I was self-conscious of a patch of skin on my face that had become affected. Each time my wife pointed out a new spot, I downplayed it.

"Could it be leprosy?" she suggested. "Shouldn't you get it checked out just in case?"

The more she worried, the more I downplayed it, but inside I was beginning to worry that she may be right. Week after week, I stubbornly refused to follow up on the appointments that my wife made for me. Finally, I went to a doctor, still partly in denial, but also wanting to get her off of my back and hopeful to get a clean bill of health.

"You have leprosy." The doctor's frank words created more fear for this battle-hardened general than any opponent I had faced in war.

This was dreaded news in my day, with few options for treatment and a stigma that would follow. In Israel, they made people call themselves unclean and avoid the general population, sometimes relegating them to a life of solitude and seclusion. Thankfully I lived in Syria, with fewer restrictions. That did not change the reality, however; and I knew I faced a long and gradual loss of function and an early retirement from my successful military career.

I reluctantly told my wife what the doctor said, but then promptly tried to focus on other things. After all, there were battles to be fought and parades to march in, and the king would not understand if Naaman, his number one general was not there. I could not appear weak. I had to keep up an image of strength. I found ways to cover the parts of my skin that would reveal my condition. I avoided situations that would make me vulnerable to others knowing my condition.

Only my wife knew—or so I thought.

"You told her?" I screamed at my wife. "What were you thinking? How dare you insult me by letting our servant girl know that I have leprosy?"

I knew they had become too close. Servants needed to be kept at a distance to let them know their position. How embarrassing that she would be privy to such information.

I was enraged. I had lost control at my wife once again. It didn't help when she defended her action by saying that this girl was the only person she had to talk to in my frequent absences. Now she was implying that I was in denial. It made me so angry when my wife suggested that I was gone too much.

What can you expect? I am a general!

When she saw that I had gotten it all out of my system and had calmed down a bit, my wife went on to tell me that this Hebrew girl knew some prophet of God in Israel who could do miracles and perhaps cure me.

The audacity of a servant girl to tell a general what to do about a problem. She had no business even knowing about my situation in the first place.

I did everything I could to avoid letting my wife see a new boil or patch of leprosy. Every time she did, she reminded me about the prophet who may be able to help me. Despite my pride and stubbornness, my condition was getting worse, and I knew I had to seek help.

If I needed to get help, then I would seek counsel from my king. If he told me to go, I would be listening to a king's orders and not my wife's—or worse yet, a servant girl.

The king was very supportive. In fact, he told me that he wanted me to go to this prophet and see if he could help. I was too valuable to lose, he stated; and to help avoid any potential problems in entering the country, he wanted to send me with a letter from himself to the king of Israel.

This gave me confidence that I was on the right track. I gathered up a generous number of gifts to present to the prophet, secured the letter within my robe, and was on my way. Perhaps there was hope. I was stepping out of denial. I was ready for help.

While I was not expecting the reception of an old friend, considering the history of our two nations, I was not fully prepared for the reaction of the king of Israel when he flew into a rage. He even tore his robe in frustrated anger and dismay, all the while going on about us trying to start a war!

How do you get trying to start a war from a friendly letter humbly asking for introduction to a prophet to help a general receive healing?

Talk about misunderstandings! Apparently, what was supposed to be a request to meet a prophet turned into a direct demand for healing.

The king of Israel took this to mean that my king was asking him to do the impossible and setting him up for war. A lot of anger results when people feel they are being asked to do what they cannot. We are even more susceptible to anger when we think the worst of people's intentions. This king was red hot!

People notice this kind of anger, and word travels fast when it's the king who is displaying it! Soon, the prophet (the very one who I was supposedly sent to see) sent word to the king to send me his way and he would help.

His response was calm. It takes a calm response to deal with an angry person effectively. He told the king that this was not an obstacle to fear but an opportunity to embrace. This was a chance to demonstrate God's power to heal to someone who did not know God like he did.

What a relief. The king calmed down, mumbled a sort of half-hearted apology about a misunderstanding, and gave me a military escort to the prophet Elisha's house.

I pulled up in my chariot, driven by multiple horses and accompanied by some of my closest officers. While still unsure of whether this would help, I was becoming hopeful. I also was looking forward to meeting this famous prophet who I was hearing about. Perhaps he would bow in reverence for my position. Perhaps he would wave his hand over me and pray to his God in a moving prayer that would be worthy of my status.

Surely he had heard of me and would be honored that I had come all this way for his services. A man like me would be great publicity for his future healing practice! With these thoughts running through my head, I waited as one of my officers went to the door and let Elisha's assistant know of my arrival. Any moment now, Elisha would appear and the ceremony would begin.

Contrary to all my expectations, the servant came out with no fanfare, just a message from the prophet telling me to go and wash off in the muddy Jordan River seven times and I would be healed. I don't know which made me more irate—the fact that the prophet did not as much as walk out to acknowledge me or the repulsive idea of washing in this poor excuse for a river.

I lost it! This was not what I had come all this way for, what I expected, or certainly, what I deserved. We had much more respectable, cleaner, larger rivers back home. What a waste of my time to come and be treated with such little respect. I got in my chariot and took off in a disgusted rage.

Well, as usual, it took me a few minutes, but my blood pressure went back to normal, and my thinking became a little more rational. With my patient officers who had seen me like this on several occasions, I was soon convinced that as strange as it sounded, it was worth a chance. What harm would it do to try? What if this was the only way for me to be healed? Didn't I owe it to myself and all those who came with me to at least give it a try?

After some major coaxing, my advisers won over my stubborn will and we were headed down to the banks of the Jordan River. I cringed as I stepped hesitantly into the muddy water. There was nothing inviting or refreshing about this river. I hoped that this scene of the great Syrian general stripped of his regal garments and immersing himself into these cloudy waters would not be relayed to others upon our return.

After dipping half-heartedly into the water a couple of times, I paused to examine my skin. Nothing had changed. It appeared futile, a waste of time. After a little more coaxing by my patient officers who knew me all too well, I continued, this time more intentionally—a third, fourth, fifth, and a sixth time.

With each dip, I was doing what I was supposed to be doing. With each dip, I was releasing some of the pride that had held me in bondage of what others thought and of how I appeared. I was obeying, but even after six dips, nothing had changed. Should I bother trying one more time? Is this really going to work? I had come this far, and now I was determined to give it my all. I took that seventh dip.

Even before I had come up out of that water, I knew something was different about this last time. Something like scales had fallen off and were floating in the water. As I touched my skin to see what was happening, it felt like a baby's skin, soft and pure. I was clean, despite having been in the muddiest water I had stepped foot in since childhood.

I began to laugh; I admit it. I splashed and shouted and laughed—just a like a child.

I have often wondered what would have happened if I had held onto my pride and refused to dip in that dirty water. Or what if I had stopped and given up before my miracle? What if I had followed instructions for the first six steps and failed to take the seventh? Not only would I have lived a short life and dealt with years of unnecessary pain and embarrassment, but I may never have come to know the God who had that power to heal and to give me a new lease on life!

Still giddy with excitement and unfazed by what anyone thought of me, I hurried back to the prophet's house.

"Don't we need to start heading back now to get home before dark?" one of the officers asked.

"There is always time to express gratitude to those who deserve it," I replied, to the surprise of those who were not used to Naaman stopping to give others credit.

This time, I did not care whether the prophet came to the door or not. All those self-serving expectations and grandiose thoughts had gotten me nowhere. It was the willingness to let go of my way and to embrace this message of humble surrender that had brought my healing. I was determined to make some changes, to change my focus, and to accept the unexpected from the hand of the unexplainable.

I was choosing faith, and I had no intention of returning to the angry existence of my past. It was time to let go and to embrace life on God's terms.

I bowed humbly before the prophet, grateful for the miracle I had received, and urged him to receive my generous gifts in return. "Not necessary," he insisted. He was simply a servant, doing as God led and giving of what God provided. He expected nothing in return. What a contrast he was to my constant need for recognition and personal glory.

I determined then and there that I was no longer living for Naaman or Naaman's glory. I wanted to serve this same God that Elisha served, that my servant girl served. It was time to let go of my idols, including that idol of pride and personal gain.

I confessed to Elisha the prophet my newfound faith and my intentions of following this God. My confession was for myself as much as for anyone, but it also meant that as I shared it out loud in front of those who came with me, it would be harder for me to go back on it. I was declaring my intentions in front of others, to walk a different path. I knew how easy it would be when I was back alone with my old crowd to return to my old ways. I needed them to know of my intentions as well. I then asked Elisha for permission to load up some soil from this sacred place to carry back. I needed reminders of this day, and I could not go back to life as it was.

I even went a step further and began to make a plan for how I would stay on this path. I will not bow down to the old idols, the meaningless substitutes for the God of heaven. I will only worship the one true God, the Higher Power who had healed the old me and given me a new start. I also knew that I needed to have accountability with this man, my "sponsor" in my new life.

I told him exactly where and how I would be vulnerable to relapse. I had to accompany the king I served to his house of worship and it would have been easy for me to get caught back up into the old life. As part of my duty, I was expected to accompany him and to help him up and down as he worshipped, but I was declaring here to this man and to all of those who were going to see me in that other setting that I would not worship those idols. If they saw me kneeling, it would only be in assisting him, and I would maintain these boundaries for my spiritual recovery.

It seemed strange that soon after I left, Elisha's servant came and said that Elisha had changed his mind and that he needed some of those gifts after all. He said something about some needy prophets he wanted to bless.

While I thought it odd and had some suspicions about this servant's manner in asking, I took him at his word and complied. I was done with a life of trying to take everyone else's inventory! The only life I needed to examine was my own. This man was responsible to God and not to me.

I was glad for the long journey home. While I was not responsible for Elisha's servant, I had an inventory to do of my own. I had been arrogant in how I dealt with my men. I had been selfish in the little time I gave to my wife. I had lost my temper with our servants, my own family, and numerous individuals who failed to meet my expectations. I had a few amends to make upon my return.

"Honey, I am so sorry for how I have treated you," I said, wasting no time as I walked in the door. I was determined to make amends for it all.

We talked into the early hours of the next morning as I shared all that had happened on this trip and of my newfound faith in my Higher Power. My wife smiled, confessing that she had come to believe in this God as well, thanks to the little girl who I had brought home from battle—this same girl that had pointed me to the prophet in Israel.

I still struggle at times when I start to focus on what I have no control over or what others think of me, how someone failed to meet my expectations, or when my pride starts to raise its ugly head. I do well again, however, when I let go of those expectations of control and take it one day and one moment at a time.

One of the most important things I do on a daily basis is to kneel on that soil that I brought back from the prophet's house. I really had no idea where I was going to place that and what I was going to do with it. I first thought that I would find a spot in the backyard where nobody would see it and nobody would question me about it. I decided instead to put it outside the front entrance so that everyone would know and so that I would have constant accountability. It is also an important reminder every time that I start to forget or begin to think that maybe things weren't so bad back then.

I need reminders. I must never forget. Life with leprosy—without healing, without God—was a miserable existence. It was through that horrible disease of leprosy that I was able to see my true brokenness and come to know the only Higher Power, and for this I will always be grateful. May you also find the freedom that comes with surrender and the joy that comes in serving him! Thank you for allowing me to share my story with you.

Questions for Reflection:

1. Share if you have had a challenge like Naaman's leprosy that humbled you and how that felt.
2. Unmet expectations feed anger. What were some of Naaman's unmet expectations that flew him into a rage? What are yours?
3. Who else in this story became angry, and what was behind the anger?
4. What did it look like for Naaman to finally surrender his will to God's care and control? What would that look like for you?
5. Naaman had some amends to make after his change of heart. Share if you have had to make amends after you began your recovery.
6. The author uses some imagination in suggesting what happened with that soil that Naaman took back. Regardless of what he used it for, what do you think is significant about having something to help remind you of past victories? What could be a reminder for you?

Principles for Recovery:

1. Until you hit bottom, you may not look up.
2. Unspoken expectations are a setup for unleashed anger.
3. Recovery is more than one step. Don't stop short!
4. Marking your recovery will help you maintain it.
5. When you no longer need the recognition of man, you are ready for the rewards of God.

Crushed but Not Defeated

(Job's Story)

Some of you may have heard my name before. Maybe you even know some of the behind-the-scenes coverage that came out in my book. What I wasn't aware of at the time was that there was quite a spiritual battle going on over my faith. All I knew was that my fantastic life almost instantly came crashing down around me with heart-wrenching devastation and unbearable loss. Through it all, I remained a grateful believer despite having gone through an intense period filled with doubt and despair. My name is Job.

I was blessed with a good home, and my children were close, even as adults. They got along so well that the seven boys would take turns hosting an event at one of their homes, and everyone was always invited. Every occasion was a celebration—with some celebrations lasting days. I was intentional in my prayer life. I took time each morning to commune with God, to give thanks, and to intercede on behalf of each of my children. I did not want any of them going astray. Their spiritual state was very important to me.

We never worried about having enough because we were considered among the wealthiest members of the community. We had plenty of oxen to plow our fields, sheep for wool, and meat for our table, along with donkeys and camels that we raised and traded for whatever else we needed.

I was grateful for all that God had provided. I let others know that these were the gifts of God, and it was not of our own merit that we were so blessed. Obviously, it took a lot of employees to run our place, and I was thankful for good workers. I made sure to treat them well.

My wife enjoyed the finer things of our day, and while giving lip service to faith, she was often more engaged in the material world than the spiritual. She gave God credit for what we had, but I sometimes wondered how her faith would fare in the event of a loss or setback. We were soon to find out.

It was another ordinary afternoon, or so it seemed. I was sitting at home with my wife, enjoying the view from the front porch, and the kids had let us know they were having one of their feasts together at our oldest son's home. He was always so generous in having his six younger brothers and three younger sisters over and provided plenty for all. I was proud of him—proud of all of them!

All of the sudden, I saw a runner. I had never seen someone running as fast and hard as the young man coming our way. He tried to catch his breath as he relayed the somber news. Enemy raiders had come onto the property, stolen all of the oxen and donkeys, and killed all of the farmhands. He was the only one left and had taken off as soon as it happened.

I had no time to even fully process this news. Another messenger suddenly approached with the same intensity and with a look of terror in his eyes. "Your sheep and shepherds were hit by a sudden lightning strike and all were destroyed. It barely missed me!" I couldn't comprehend what was happening.

Before that messenger could even finish, a third had come out of who knows where and was relaying the loss of all our camels. My mind was spinning. *At least the kids were safe at the home of our oldest*, I thought.

I was trying to digest all this—what it meant to our livelihood, our home, and our property. Then suddenly one more bearer of bad news arrived.

This man conveyed the worst news of all. A tornado had swept through the house where the kids had gathered. I held my breath, afraid to ask if they had survived. There was no doubt, he continued, that they were all lost.

My wife wailed in agony. My heart split in two. It felt as if someone was holding a knife to my chest. I tore my robe, shaved my head, and fell to the ground. I ached to the core. I could not imagine life without our dear children. The livestock were replaceable, but not our kids! It was utterly devastating.

Despite the shock and the loss that had just hit me, I was reminded that my faith was not in the things that God had given me but in the God who had given them to me. I came into this world without anything. Everything I had was a gift of grace, undeserved.

"The Lord gave me what I had, and the Lord has taken it away. Praise the name of the Lord!" I declared.

Though I did not understand it and though it would take me time to process the magnitude of what I had lost, I fully believed my declaration. God deserves praise at all times, regardless of our current state of events. My wife shook her head and appeared to glare at me while beating the ground. I lay there bowed before the Lord, searching my heart for answers but continuing to praise him.

In the days following, I reminisced about the earlier years with the children. I thanked God for each memory and sometimes couldn't stop crying as I missed them so much. Having ten children did not take away from the unique individuality and blessings that each provided. I had no idea how life could continue without them. I was not sure I wanted it to. Nothing would be the same.

Back and forth between grief and praise, my faith in the Lord helped me cope with what felt unbearable some days. My wife said little and seemed to operate in a catatonic state of mere existence. She had no use for my prayers or declarations of praise to a God who she was coming to resent. She was inconsolable. My continued faith was often the target of her anger and bitterness.

Just when it seemed that nothing worse could take place and that I had nothing more to lose, it happened. I went to bed thinking of my children yet thanking God that at least I had my health. Then I awoke to some of the most intense pain I had ever experienced.

No matter which way I turned, it felt like someone or something was tearing into my skin. What began as a few spots on each side soon evolved into aching, itching, excruciatingly painful boils covering my body. I went outside and picked up an old broken pot, pressing it against the boils, scraping, and hoping to bring relief. Soon I was covered from my head to my toes.

My wife walked over with a look of dismay. Maybe she could offer me some hope, comfort, or even a glass of water to bring relief. Instead, what she offered was the most discouraging form of "advice" I had ever received.

"God has abandoned you," she said. "There is no use trusting him any longer. Renounce your faith, curse God, and take your own life. You have nothing more to live for!"

Had I heard her right? Was my own wife telling me to die? I knew she was struggling with God after losing all that we had lost, but I still did not see this coming. I had wondered at times if her faith was more about what God could do for us than the reality that he was God and worthy of praise. I always hoped, however, that with a little testing and stretching, her faith would become stronger. It was now evident that what faith she once had was no longer evident and that what the testing had done was to reveal what was missing and not what was there.

"You are speaking foolishly!" I reprimanded her. "God is God regardless of what he does or does not do for us. We need to accept both the things we consider good and the things we consider bad as from God."

I don't know if I was speaking these things so much for her benefit as a reminder to myself, to lean on those things I knew to be true. I chose this path even as I saw her becoming full of bitterness and disgust.

Trials are hardest when we bear them alone. I watched my wife walk away. I sat aching, physically and emotionally, feeling all alone for what felt like an eternity. I began to wonder if anyone cared or if I had anyone left.

Then three friends arrived—men from backgrounds different than mine and whose friendship with me went way back. We had laughed together, cried with one another, shared dreams, and carried each other's burdens. These were three friends who knew when to show up and how to just sit with me—for a while at least.

I knew it was them before they got close. They, on the other hand, were not sure it was me because the boils had begun to distort my face. I tried to meet them but could barely stand. Each time my weight pressed into the sores on my feet, the pain was unbearable. I sat and waited for them.

Finally my friends recognized me as they got closer. When they did, they all tore their robes and threw dust over themselves, identifying with me in my pain and agony. Solidarity with brothers felt like such a welcome relief.

For seven days, nobody said a word. Their silence spoke volumes. They cried with me. Their presence was powerful. They later told me they did not know what to say. In reality, those first seven days were the most helpful of their entire stay.

They gave me the greatest gift of all—the gift of just being there with me. I knew they did not have to stay. I knew they had other places they could be and had other people in their lives. But in those days of silence, their presence told me that I mattered to them, that my pain mattered to them, and that they cared!

After feeling safe, and thinking they cared, I was the one who broke the silence. I lamented this painful existence. I regretted the day I was born. I expressed my deep sorrow, pain, and loss. I shared my frustration and the fact that none of what I had been

118 • PAUL BISHOP

through made sense. I held nothing back. I knew God could handle my true state, and I mistakenly thought my friends could as well.

I was right about God, but sadly, wrong about my friends.

Soon, they felt obligated to press me on what sins I had committed to bring this horrible state upon myself. They said that by not admitting that I was being punished for something and by not renouncing whatever that sin was, I was discrediting our faith. It wasn't easy hearing them accuse me. It's not like I had not had time to examine my life and do an inventory of any areas I had left unconfessed.

Truth is, I had honestly been keeping a daily inventory of my life. There was nothing that had built up that could have caused God to do this to me. They, however, thought otherwise. And they felt the need to tell me so!

Eliphaz started by expressing respect for how I had been used of God to encourage others. However, he suddenly added in the dreaded, "BUT . . . "

"Now when trouble strikes, you lose heart!" he accused. Instead of encouragement, his words became an accusation suggesting I was weak and lacked faith. According to him, if I had done no wrong, I should have nothing to fear.

"Stop and think," he continued. "Do the innocent die?"

I wanted to reply that yes, they actually do. What planet have they been living on? Life is not fair. Good people do suffer. Things are never so black and white as they seemed to believe.

Eliphaz had some good things to say. He talked about how, though God wounds, he also bandages. He talked about how being corrected by God is a good thing. Just because those are true, however, did not mean that those facts applied to my situation.

Bildad and Zophar followed with their perspective and also had some truth in the mix of what they said. The problems stemmed from what they assumed, the way in which they presented it, and their judgmental attitudes.

I don't know which was worse anymore—sitting there with boils that kept me awake at night and miserable all day or sitting and listening to my three codependent friends! They wanted so badly to fix my situation, to fix me! At one point my sarcastic nature took over and I retorted, "You people really know everything, don't you? And when you die, wisdom will die with you! Well, I know a few things myself, and you're no better than I am!" (Job 12:1-2)

Later I told them, "If only you could be silent! That's the wisest thing you could do! Be silent now and leave me alone. Let me speak, and I will face the consequences!" (13:5,13)

Yes, I smelled codependency all over these guys. Somehow, they thought if they tried hard enough or talked long enough, they could convince me that they were right and that I was wrong. They thought it was up to them to protect me from some dire consequences that would come from my complaints and "lack of repentance."

Bildad asked, "How long will you go on like this? You sound like a blustering wind!"

I could have asked him the same question. I couldn't help wondering how he would have been doing if he was in my sandals.

Zophar asked, "Can you solve the mysteries of God? Can you discover everything about the Almighty?" (Job 11:7)

I knew the answer to that—of course I cannot. But he sure thought he knew a lot and somehow thought he could set me straight since he knew God better, apparently, than I did.

Eliphaz said, "You are nothing but a windbag!" (Job 15:2) *Speak for yourself, Eliphaz.*

He also asked, "Is God's comfort too little for you?"

While I agonized over God's silence, it was sure more comforting than their accusations and attempts to fix me and my situation! In fact, I went ahead and told them they were all miserable comforters! I told them that if the roles were reversed, I would be offering comfort and not condemnation.

It is hard to be falsely accused. It is even harder to listen to your kids be falsely accused. I had prayed for them often and taught them well, and I was proud of how they had turned out. I could not believe it when Bildad so boldly suggested that my children must have sinned against God, "so their punishment was well deserved!"

I would put my kids' reputation and innocence against these guys and their families any day. How dare he suggest they deserved this! They had their issues, but my children confessed their sins and lived lives of integrity. They each took their own inventory—unlike these guys who were taking everyone else's and not their own.

In between these guys' talking and accusing, I must admit I also had a lot to say. None of us would have made it in a group where there was a guideline about keeping your sharing to three to five minutes. None of us were very good at keeping our sharing focused on ourselves either!

It was not easy to keep my inventory balanced as they poured out negativity and attempts at shaming me. But I refused to take on shame or feelings of guilt for things of which I was being accused just because it was being spoken around me.

I reminded myself of how I had learned to "bounce my eyes" and avoid indulging in lust. I recalled my attempts to be fair to my servants and how I treated them with respect. Unlike many around me, I saw them as my equals, all part of God's creation. I made sure that I had looked out for those less fortunate than myself, provided clothing for the homeless, and made provision for widows and orphans in my community. Despite having been blessed with wealth, I did not place trust in that wealth and did not flaunt it to others.

No, even after a careful inventory, I did not see cause for my suffering. I knew I was not perfect. In fact, when I did wrong, I promptly admitted it and made amends for it. I did not pretend to be better than I was, unlike some people (but I will not mention any names—I would hate to embarrass Bildad, Zophar, or Eliphaz!).

Regardless of what I was being told, I knew that what I was experiencing was not judgment for something I had done. I still hurt and still did not understand, but I was going to continue to place my trust in the God who does understand. God knew what was going on, even when I did not.

I chose to consider this a test, knowing that, in his hands, I would come out stronger on the other end.

I almost forgot to mention that there was one other guy who showed up that day. I don't know exactly when Elihu came. When you're going through trials, you lose track of time.

I give Elihu credit for being able to sit still and listen longer than the others. Honestly, I can't say I remember much of his long speech, but I do know that, despite his efforts to explain God, he had the same wrong theology as the others. He seemed to genuinely believe that if people simply obey God, "they will be blessed with prosperity throughout their lives." What a sad distortion of reality.

Just when I was about to tell these four guys to please leave and let me sit in my own misery—just when I was thinking that I had all I could take and had reached my limit—at just the right time, God showed up!

Interestingly, God did not answer my many questions or tell me why I was put through so much testing. He did tell my friends that I had spoken more accurately than they had. That felt good to hear!

But he gave me some questions to think about too, and I suddenly realized I had been far too arrogant. Though I was not being punished for a particular sin, I had become prideful.

Who was I to demand that God answer my questions?

Who was I to judge my friends—even if their words were incredibly hurtful.

Who was I to focus so much on myself that I lose sight of my creator and his wider perspective on all things?

After God opened my eyes to his wonders and reminded me who he is, I said little. I was done with long speeches. I was done with religious eloquence! I had no need to justify or prove anything to God or to anyone else. The most important thing was that my faith was now not just based upon what I had heard but upon what I had seen. God's presence had overshadowed all of my so-called knowledge of him.

As I sat and listened to God, my own pain, as real as it still was, paled and dimmed in light of his glory. My reality had not changed, but my awareness of his reality had. I bowed in reverence and asked for forgiveness.

Hours earlier, I might have gloated over what happened next. In my sarcasm and pride, I would have enjoyed hearing God say that I had more accurately presented a view of his nature than the ones portrayed by my friends. But I had changed in the light of sitting in the very presence of God.

He told my friends they needed to make amends to God and me by presenting offerings and by asking me to pray for their forgiveness.

What an amazing experience that was to pray for these friends and to be God's instrument in their healing. I had often prayed for my family and for forgiveness for myself. But getting down on my knees next to these men who had been my accusers and asking God to forgive and restore them was when something amazing began.

I no longer felt resentment for all the hurtful things they had said in those long speeches. I began to feel a lightness within my heavy heart that I had not felt since these tragedies had begun. I even began to notice the lingering boils were no longer painful as I focused all my energy on praying for the restoration of these friends.

Soon, my brothers and sisters, as well as other friends, came to see me and brought comfort for all I had experienced. I am not sure where they were when I needed them the most, but that is OK. I am not here to do their inventory. I am done with judgment and sarcasm. I am choosing to live in freedom!

I could tell you so much more. I could tell you how God restored and doubled all that I had before. I could tell you about my second lease on life and more children whom I was blessed to raise.

But focusing too much on that would take away from the most important lesson I learned—faith is NOT about understanding the "why" or the "how." It is coming to know the "who." I am blessed not because I have these valuable possessions or even relationships, but because I am privileged to know the Creator of all things. He is my source, my strength, and my deliverer.

Thank you for letting me share!

Questions for Reflection:

1. What was happening behind the scenes that Job did not know about?
2. How were Job's views of suffering challenged? When have you had your views of suffering or of God challenged through your experience?
3. Why do you think that Job's friends didn't speak for seven days?
4. Why did Job call his friends "miserable comforters?" Share when you may have had a similar experience of being "comforted" by well-meaning friends.
5. Why did God make Job pray for his friends? What happened when he did?
6. What is your takeaway from Job's experience regarding faith and pain?

Principles for Recovery:

1. Friends offer more in their silence than in their sermons.
2. Accepting the things you cannot change will help you focus on the things that you can.
3. The presence of God changes the perspective of man.
4. Praying for those who hurt you prepares for God to heal you.

Running with Nowhere to Hide

(Jonah's Story)

I am a survivor of deep-sea trauma. Though a believer in almighty God, I still struggle with pride, anger, and prejudice. My name is Jonah. I grew up in a town called Gath Hepher in the territory of Zebulon in the northern kingdom of Israel. That may not mean a lot to you, but it certainly does to me, as I grew up quite proud of my heritage.

For many years I served God faithfully, and from the outside, I appeared to be a compliant and humble servant. I successfully predicted the expansion of my nation's territory during the leadership of King Jeroboam II. It gave me great joy to see my country prospering. As long as my country was doing well and I was able to do what I enjoyed, I felt good about myself and my life. I was proud to be one of God's chosen people, and on top of that, to be a prophet that others looked up to as the voice of God. Things were going well in my life.

One day when I was daydreaming about what my next assignment might be and of what great manner in which God was going to use me to further help my people, I was given the unexpected message from God that he wanted me to go to the town of Nineveh, the capital of the Assyrians, to call upon them for repentance.

I thought for sure that I must have heard God wrong. Surely he would not expect me to go there, of all places. Those people had been our enemies and were trying to take over our country. I hate to admit it, but I have spent years despising those folks. Just the thought of going there triggered a lot of my bitterness and anger toward them. No way would I lower myself to go to that place.

Despite my best efforts, I did not change God's mind, and sadly, he did not change mine. He was determined to send me to Nineveh. I was determined not to go. I did what every human being from the beginning of time has tried to do when faced with having God tell him which way to turn: I went the other direction! I went down to the local port and found a ship going the very opposite direction—to Tarsus. Call me ignorant, but I thought that if he saw me going the opposite direction, God would leave me alone and be done with me. This was not the case!

As soon as the ship left port, I found a good spot in the hold to get away and get some sleep. It can be exhausting, fighting with God. I was tired, drained, and empty within. I needed to get away from my merry shipmates. I was at a low point emotionally and spiritually, and I just wanted to be left alone to get some rest. Sleep was the one thing that I thought would help me feel better.

Every waking moment I remembered God's voice, wondering if he hated me for my response. I grieved over no longer having that sense of closeness that I used to enjoy with God. While I was relieved to not be going to Nineveh, I was also stuck on a boat full of other messed up people with strange views about God. I did not feel like I could relate to these people and was glad to find an isolated spot to get some rest. Sometimes the loneliest place is in a crowd full of people. At other points of my life, I may have seen this crowd on the boat as an opportunity to represent God to lost individuals. At this point, all I could hope for was some escape and relief from reality.

I had barely fallen asleep when I was roughly awakened by other sailors telling me to get up there and help the rest of the crew throw out excess supplies and try to lighten the load of the ship. It turned out that we had come upon some severe weather and the ship was out of control. I had been on the sea on numerous occasions, but never had I seen it like this. The sailors began crying out to their various gods and pleading for help. Nothing seemed to work. Nobody's god seemed to listen.

As I heard them pleading to these empty gods, I realized that the only god who had the power to calm this sea was the God who created it in the first place. Any other time in my life, I would have been the first to cry out to my God. I would have begged him for mercy and would have welcomed the chance to speak to him. Today was a different story. I had rejected him, run from him, and rebelled from his calling on my life. He had not left me, but I had left him.

How could I call on him? How could I ask for his help? In fact, this whole predicament was probably a result of my behavior. Perhaps God was punishing me or trying to get my attention, and now all these people were suffering for my poor choices. Yes, how many times our poor choices affect those around us! I came to realize that I was powerless to run from God, and only the true Higher Power could help any of us survive this ordeal.

"Throw me overboard!" I screamed at the top of my lungs. The waves were getting louder and nobody seemed to hear me. "Throw me overboard now!" I repeated, just as a crash of thunder interrupted my cry.

The men thought they had not heard me correctly until I repeated myself again, then explained that I was running from the true God of the universe and that I believed that this storm was a consequence of my poor choices. I let them know that I was convinced that the storm would die down once they got me out of the boat. They hesitated, showing a compassion for me that I did not feel toward them or any other people different than me. With reluctance, they concurred, and soon I felt myself failing deep into the depths of the sea before my body began to come back up to the surface again.

The sea became eerily quiet. Beyond the sloshing water against the boat that was now becoming more and more distant, I could hear cries of praise to the Creator. Perhaps even in my rebellion, the true Higher Power of the universe had been able to use me to display who he is. Perhaps he was even now capable of salvaging and using the pieces of my life for good! Perhaps he was not done with me.

The thought gave me a faint hope, but my mind was soon back to reality as I fought to stay above the waterline and my body struggled to navigate the waves. It soon became apparent that I had nothing more to give and that my limp arms and legs could battle the water no more. My body was descending deep into the sea, and it felt like I was about to meet my very Maker whom I had disobeyed. I needed to pray but struggled to breathe and felt seaweed about to strangle me around my neck. Just as I was about to swallow one last gallon of water, I faced a sea creature larger and closer than anything I had ever encountered. I was sure that this was it! My time of reckoning was here. I was terrified.

I wondered if this was my final judgment and my final destiny, to be attacked, chewed up, and spit out by an angry sea monster. If so, this was just. I had let down the one who had changed my life. I deserved death. Part of me even cried out for it, but even as I braced myself—even as I saw glimpses of teeth that were larger and more terrifying than anything I had seen—it became dark. I was still alive and safely in the inner cavities of a large animal.

What appeared to be my greatest source of terror and destruction now appeared to be my greatest source of deliverance and security. I was safe from the turmoil. I could breathe again. I did not particularly enjoy my surroundings, and I certainly did not find the odors appealing, but what a relief to catch my breath and to know that I was somehow still alive! Relief was mixed with reality. I was somehow in the belly of a large sea creature. I was bound to be destroyed by its digestive juices as I would soon descend through its intestines and be pushed down through its bowels and—never mind, I couldn't even go there.

I began to beg God for another chance.

I had been foolish. I had been prideful. I had forgotten who was in charge. I had taken on the role of being the higher power in my own life. "Oh God, if only you would allow me another chance!" I began to bargain, to plead, and to make promises. If I somehow would get out of this creature alive, I would never run from God again. I would do whatever he wanted me to do.

I would even go to Nineveh. I couldn't believe I had just said that, but when you are desperate, things change, and you find yourself making promises you never thought you would make and willing to do things you never thought you would be willing to do. When the pain of staying where you are becomes greater than the pain of the change itself, you are ready to do anything. You have fully embraced the need for change. I still did not like Nineveh, and I still preferred to make my own decisions, but it obviously had not worked out too well doing it my way, and I was ready to surrender my life and my will to his care and control. Walking through Nineveh would be better than a slow death inside of this monster.

Was it too late? Did God hear me? Did he still want to use me?

As unexpectedly as I had faced those fearsome jaws and been swallowed alive, I felt the muscles of this creature tighten and heard the sounds of vomiting bellowing up within it. Before I could even tell you for sure what was happening, I was ejected back up a narrow and dark passageway and toward the light. I was ejected through the open mouth of this sea monster onto dry land. Every muscle in my being ached—from the jostling in the creature's belly, the muscles constricted around me, the hours of being tossed on the ship.

The only thing worse than how I felt at that moment was probably how I looked! As I stopped to ask the first person I saw which was the way to Nineveh, his look of shock and fear reminded me that I must have been a sight for sore eyes! As I got closer to town, I heard one little boy ask his mom, "Why does that strange man smell like that, Mommy?"

At this point, the gratefulness I felt to be alive and the anticipation I felt for how God was going to use me to help him bring justice to the people of Nineveh was enough to overcome my fear of what anyone thought of my appearance. Seeing a few of the small children clinging to their parents as I approached awakened a bit of compassion within as I thought about the pending destruction they would experience.

That feeling quickly passed, however, when I saw a couple of hardened men standing on the street corners, reminding me of the violent and inhumane manner in which they had dealt with my people over the years.

As I walked through town and relived some of the memories of what had happened to my people, anger and old resentments stirred up inside of me. I remembered stories of rape, assault, and violent abuse. I began to anticipate what God would do to these people and had a new adrenaline that drove me from street corner to street corner, as I let people know that God was angry with them and that time was running out. I felt that my anger was also justified. After all, didn't these people deserve judgment?

My recent experience of undeserved grace and the second chance that allowed me to be standing here was quickly forgotten. I felt quite smug in my own religiosity as I preached to these heathens who were doomed and destined for judgment any day. *Thank God I am not like those people*, I said to myself.

After I had made it up and down the streets, I looked for a good and safe location where I could await the destruction and see the heathen citizens of Nineveh go up in flames. As I left the city, I heard some weeping, and as I turned around, I saw people dressed in sackcloth and covered with ashes.

This was how people in my day showed their remorse and regrets or extreme feelings of sadness and grief. Surely this was too little too late, however, to change the impending judgment that they all so clearly deserved. Surely God would see through some petty attempts at seeking his mercy and forgiveness after years and years of terrible behaviors. Surely.

I found my spot. It was far enough away to be safe from flying embers or the potential heat to come but also close enough to see the destructive force when it hit. I rationalized my desire to watch this not as revenge but as righteous anger and a desire for justice to prevail. I pushed aside my fears that God would somehow change his mind or forgive the people of Nineveh for their despicable acts. I began to anticipate the damnation to come. I knew that regardless of anything that I had done, everyone in that city had done far worse.

I tried to block out the memories of the old women and the small children tagging along with fear in their eyes as I spoke of the judgment to come. After all, they were all part of this and guilty by association. I blocked out the nagging thoughts of the mercy I had received and the mistakes I had made. After all, how much worse it must be to worship false gods than to disobey the real one?

I waited forty days, and the deadline for judgment on the city of Nineveh approached. Today the world would see what God thought of the likes of these Assyrians. Today the people of Israel would be vindicated for all the wrongs that had been committed against them. Today people would know that I was a true prophet of God. After today, people around the world would know that Jonah was the man, and when Jonah speaks, people would now listen.

This was going to be the beginning of something big. I waited in anticipation—and I waited . . . and waited . . . and waited some more. The day passed and I began to recalculate. Perhaps the days had become a blur for me. Perhaps it had only been thirty-nine days. I waited the next day, just in case. And I waited again. Nothing happened. I could hear the sound of singing and saw glimpses of people dancing in the streets of Nineveh.

The louder the singing, the madder I became. The more animated the dancing, the more agitated I felt. I began to feel a despair unlike anything I had known before. When I felt like I may not make it inside the sea creature's belly, I at least felt like I deserved it. Now I was angrier and angrier because I felt how unfair this world was and how much those people down there celebrating should not be here. They should be facing judgment, burning in hell, receiving the consequences of their actions.

I should have been the one celebrating their destruction. I was the one who deserved to be happy. If this is how life was, I wanted out. I did not want to be here anymore.

Once again, when I would rather have not heard his voice, God showed up. He wanted to know why I was angry. In fact, he had the audacity to ask me if I had a good reason to be angry. You better believe I did! I let him know immediately, and in no uncertain terms, that I had every right to be angry and that he had let me down. My very fear had come to pass. The people who deserved judgment were spared, were now singing and dancing, and were moving forward with their lives. The guy who had lived his whole life working hard for God (except for a few detours, such as boat rides in other directions), was now left feeling despair, disillusionment, and abandoned by the God who was supposed to be on his side, not theirs.

Well God gave me a little object lesson with a plant that grew up and offered me some shade, and just when I was beginning to think a little justice was returning to the world, a worm came and the plant withered. I was back to sitting in the hot sun, just as before, decrying my situation and full of self-pity and rehearsing the injustices I had been through. God then wanted to know why I was so upset over a little plant when he was concerned with lost individuals. He didn't seem to feel any obligation to live up to my expectations of him or to accommodate my temper tantrums regarding my comfort or the lack of fairness in this world. Then

God seemed to leave me alone, in my own thoughts to ponder all that had taken place.

Perhaps I did overreact to the plant. Perhaps it was somehow related to not having learned all I was meant to learn from my experience in the depths of the sea.

What happened next is what some call a fearless moral inventory. I began to reflect. Maybe I had been selfish in some areas. Maybe I had been prideful. Maybe I had used religion and my good deeds and efforts to make myself feel better than others. Maybe I had allowed bitterness and resentment to rob me of my own blessings that were staring me straight in the face. Maybe when God chops down one plant, it's time for me to move and find another. Maybe when God redeems someone who has repented, it's an invitation to welcome that person as a new brother or sister and recognize that this same grace that delivered me from the belly of a sea monster has been extended to another needy individual just like myself.

I was beginning to see things in a new light. In fact, I began to realize that perhaps the very painful experiences I was resenting were the ones that were bringing me to a new realization and providing a new perspective. Perhaps God had not abandoned me in any of those moments and was still there waiting to walk with me through the next.

Truth is, I began to hope again. If God could get me through those painful events, patiently teach me the lessons I needed to learn, and extend grace beyond anything I deserved, then perhaps there was a future ahead for me even yet.

I cannot say that I have arrived and never have doubts or never become angry with God. After all, my understanding of him is still limited. I cannot say I don't have nightmares of falling into the depths of the sea, and I doubt that I will ever get on a ship the rest of my life, but that's OK. I am doing better. I now wait for the bigger picture before I react. I am learning to accept the people that God has chosen who look different than me and think differently than I do.

I am even learning to forgive those who have done some horrible things to me and to those I love. After all, that is what God has done for me. And not only did God forgive me for my past attitudes and disobedience, he decided to even let me write a book—apparently it is going to be one of sixty-six just like it.

I certainly never expected to be used again, and I know that I do not deserve the second and third chances he has given me. However, I now want to spend the rest of my life sharing with others from my experiences, strength, and hope. Thank you for letting me share.

Questions for Reflection:

1. When in your time have you rebelled against God and ran the other direction?
2. What were some of your emotions and consequences from doing things your way?
3. Even after surrendering to go to Nineveh, Jonah struggled with unmet expectations of God. When have you had a similar struggle?
4. What mindset was behind Jonah's struggle with depression and anger?
5. When have you had a setback in your own recovery even after surrendering to God?
6. How do you think Jonah's story ends? Do you agree or disagree with the author's speculation?

Principles for Recovery:

1. You cannot run beyond God's reach.
2. Who you hate and what you love will define the character of who you are.

3. When you rely on temporary relief, you will end up in permanent regret.
4. An inventory of what makes you angry will reveal what you need to make you healthy.
5. The sources of your anger reveal the symptoms of your heart.

The Rock That Almost Sank

(Peter's Story)

Some remember me as the guy who walked on water. Many remember me as the guy who sank. Some think of me as a great leader, others as a great failure. As for me, I will always be humbled by my failures but grateful for my victories. I struggle with being impulsive, controlling, and putting my foot in my mouth. My name is Peter.

I grew up with my brother, Andrew, in a town called Bethsaida. Our dad, John, had a thriving fishing business and taught us how to fish, providing us with our first fishing boat. We were expected, as others in our time, to follow Dad's footsteps, and he and mom were relying more and more on us to provide for the family.

We worked in partnership with our childhood friends, James and John. The fishing business was all we knew. I got married and built a house for my family in the neighboring town of Capernaum.

I have always been someone who puts everything into whatever I do. You could say that when I am in, I am all in. I wanted to have the biggest and best fishing business on the Sea of Galilee. I compared notes when I heard of others doing well in their fishing endeavors. What bait were they using? Did they have new nets? What made the difference? How could we improve?

Andrew was a little less committed to fishing. I was a bit annoyed that he was spending less time with us on the lake instead following a strange rabbi who lived out in the desert and was talking about the Messiah to come.

Andrew kept inviting me to join him, but the fish had been biting a lot those days, and someone had to keep the nets tended to and the boat on the water. I had mouths to feed, and my parents were counting on me.

"It's about time you show up to work," I kidded Andrew as he came to where James, John, and I were fishing one day.

Andrew had something else on his mind. He shared that this rabbi he was listening to in the desert had introduced him to the coming Messiah. Andrew announced he had decided to follow him. His name was Jesus.

As Andrew talked about Jesus, I found myself becoming more and more interested in seeing what he was all about. It only helped that Andrew assured me he was not eating wild locusts and honey like the other guy we had heard about.

I told you that my name is Peter. That is true. I was not born Peter, however. I was given the name Simon. I didn't mind being called Simon, but it was a pretty common name. Sometimes I wished I had a more unique name, a name that meant something important.

It was as if Jesus knew that desire when we first met.

"Your name is Simon, John's son," Jesus rightly assessed. He then continued, "I am going to call you Peter."

"Peter," as I and everyone else standing there knew, means "rock." Everyone tried not to laugh. Nobody else would have suggested that I was anything close to being a rock. It was no secret that I could be impulsive. It was more than once that I had purchased a new boat without thinking through how we would pay for it. I was known as the guy who would step out and take a risk—but not always a calculated one.

But now a man who had never met me saw me as a "rock." I now know that he was not looking at me for who I had been but for who he saw me becoming. At that point, I did not understand it all but was glad to have a unique name. I never met another Peter in my lifetime. I will take "Peter" over "Simon" any day.

I was impressed with Jesus from the start. He was different from the other rabbi's I had met. He spoke like he knew what he was talking about. He taught like he had authority. He connected with us like he really cared and understood our lives. It probably helped that he grew up in a carpenter's shop and not spending all his time in the temple, like many of our spiritual leaders. I went out to hear him whenever I had a break from fishing, which was not often.

One day, when Andrew and I were in my boat, Jesus came walking up to us. This was more than just a friendly visit. He extended an invitation to be part of a team he was assembling of disciples that would be with him full time.

The only catch was that we had to give up fishing and travel with him wherever he was led to go. Judging from what I was hearing, this could involve a lot of walking and a lot of time away from home.

Fishing was all I knew. I would miss the sea breeze, the challenges of the catch, the joy of landing the big ones. I hesitated for just a moment.

As if he knew I loved a challenge, Jesus looked into my eyes and said, "I will teach you how to fish for people."

Wow, I could still fish, just in a different manner—something more spiritual and eternally significant.

I looked at Andrew. He was eyeing me to see what my response would be. I did not hesitate. I had given my all to fishing, but there was always a nagging doubt whether this was all there was in life. Now it was time to give this rabbi all I had. We were all in.

I guess I should have thought about who was going to run things when Andrew and I left our nets behind. Oh well, I was sure that one of our guys would come get the boat and nets when word got out that John's boys had gone fanatical and left the family business.

Yes, I was now all in with Jesus, the rabbi from Nazareth, Mary and Joseph's son. After hearing him teach and watching him perform miracles, I was convinced that he was indeed the Messiah that we were waiting for. One day he asked all of us what people were saying about him and who they thought he was.

As usual, I was the first to speak up. After answering his question about what others were saying, Jesus looked straight into my eyes, then put me on the spot.

"Who do you think I am?" he asked.

I almost surprised myself with how quickly and clearly I replied. After all, he had not told us this in so many words yet. It was something that I had grown to believe, however, and I told him and all around me what I now believed.

"You are the Messiah and the son of the living God," I blurted out. (Matthew 16:16)

This was a highlight of my journey. Jesus affirmed my declaration and reiterated that he had chosen me to be his rock. He then said something about building a church that would never be defeated and that he was giving us the keys of the kingdom. I was on cloud nine. I had nailed it.

Not only was I right about Jesus, but he really believed in me.

I had been wondering lately if I had heard Jesus wrong about me being a rock. After all, I was the guy who had stepped out of the boat to walk to Jesus, only to sink moments later. I was the one who had failed to stay afloat. I went from faith to doubt, confidence to self-condemnation in no time. This was often my experience. How could I be a rock? Perhaps Jesus knew how much I needed to hear this again so soon after sinking. It felt good to hear him say it again. This high point did not last long!

Jesus told us that even though we had come to recognize him as the Messiah, we were not to tell anyone else. He also said that as the Messiah, he was going to suffer and die at the hands of the religious leaders.

I could not take hearing him say such things. I did not want to rebuke Jesus in front of the others, so I took him aside. In fact, I did not want to rebuke him at all, but something had to be said. Not sure where his negativity was coming from, I took it on myself to set him straight and reassure him that these bad things could not happen to him.

After all, he was the Messiah.

The next words out of Jesus's mouth stung. "Get behind me, Satan!" (Matthew 16:23)

Wait, what happened to me being "the rock?" Where had this come from? Wasn't the Messiah coming to set up a new kingdom and deliver his people? I was just trying to help him along in his mission.

I still had much to learn. We all did. Jesus told me personally that I did not comprehend the spiritual element of his assignment. He then spoke to all of us and started telling us that to follow him means to give up our lives and to be willing to suffer.

A suffering Messiah? Wouldn't that mean suffering disciples? We did not realize that this was what we signed up for! Looking back, I see it now. It was part of the Old Testament prophecies. It fits with all the sacrifices for sin that we had been doing for years. But somehow, in our eagerness to embrace the final victory, we had missed the temporary battles. Our focus on ourselves had blinded us from the plan of our heavenly Father. We still didn't get it, but soon we would.

My wife was, for the most part, supportive of my many travels. It helped that we sometimes stayed at our house when passing through Capernaum. My wife was a good sport with all of those going in and out whenever Jesus stayed with us.

The most memorable visit was the time when my mother-in-law was sick and Jesus healed her. Years later, Paul spoke of the values of singleness and serving without having to be mindful of a spouse. For me, it was a blessing to be married—having a wife who not only supported my work but would sometimes accompany me as I traveled.

Being part of the team of twelve made me feel important, but being selected to join James and John as three of Jesus's inner circle meant even more. He sometimes invited us to go off by ourselves and connect a little deeper. I am pretty sure that one reason I was chosen was that he knew I needed help in learning to slow down.

One of the most memorable moments we had together was the miraculous appearance of Elijah and Moses to us on a mountainside. Jesus was literally glowing with the glory of his full divinity, and we were, mostly, speechlessly watching. Then things became a little awkward when I blurted something out in the middle of what was a super spiritual moment.

It wasn't the first time, and wouldn't be the last, that I wanted to control what was happening. I didn't want to be caught off guard. Jesus was patient with me despite my tendency to take over or to say too much. I went to sleep that night, as I did many others, asking myself why I couldn't just keep my big mouth shut!

The most difficult memories I carry as Jesus's disciple were times when I acted the least like one. As much as I believed in his position of Messiah, I failed to fully understand what his role was meant to be.

When he was washing our feet, I objected. Surely it was my place to wash his, not the other way around.

When he asked us to pray with him in the garden of Gethsemane, I didn't realize what he was facing, and I failed to even stay awake.

When his enemies showed up in the garden to arrest him, I pulled out a sword and cut off one of the soldier's ears. I could not understand why the others just stood there. Then when Jesus picked up the guy's ear and healed him, I was totally taken off guard.

Dazed and broken, I stood back and followed at a safe distance to see where they were taking Jesus. My confidence was shaken, and my faith was wavering. I had heard Jesus speak of suffering soon and of death to come, but it still had not registered that this was part of God's plan. I was not sure I was ready to be part of something like that.

As I stood watching them march Jesus before his accusers, I did not want to get too close. I did not want to meet with the same fate. I was confused about what was ahead for our cause.

I was disillusioned as to why Jesus would not fight back, as I knew he could. I was afraid for myself and began to worry over which one of us would be next. I needed to get out of there.

As I sat in the courtyard and pondered these thoughts, I was asked by one of the servants if I was not one of Jesus's followers. Fearful and looking anxiously from side to side, I vehemently denied that I knew him, and I moved slowly to the gate.

Another girl came up and started telling anyone who would listen that I was with Jesus earlier. This time I spoke strongly and swore that not only was I not with him but that I didn't even know him. I didn't want to appear too eager to leave and stayed a little longer but was becoming more fearful of who might recognize me next.

As I mingled and tried to make small talk with other bystanders, a couple of them picked up on my accent, as a Galilean, and said, "You must be one of them!"

This time I swore even more adamantly and said, "A curse on me if I'm lying—I don't know the man!"

Each lie seemed to become easier.

In the midst of my denials, I was thinking of nothing but distancing myself from Jesus to protect my own skin. I was not thinking about what I was doing or who I was hurting. Then I heard it! It was a rooster crowing! Just as it did, I caught Jesus glancing my way. I had never seen Jesus with that kind of hurt in his eyes. With that look, it all came back to me.

Jesus told me, a few days earlier, that I would deny him, just like the others. I retorted that I would never do so, even if all the others did. *No, I could never do such a thing!* What audacity to make such a claim, but I did. As the Scripture says, "If you think you are standing strong, be careful, not to fall." (1 Corinthians 10:12)

I began to weep bitterly and uncontrollably. I had never felt so low. I had failed my Messiah and dear friend. He had said it would happen. He said to be ready. He said to be in prayer. I had failed on all accounts. I slept through the prayer time. I missed the point of what was happening. Now I even denied the very one who had believed in me and had given me the name Peter. So much for being the rock! Even if he survived this ordeal, I could never face him again. I went to find the others and to warn them and perhaps receive some solace in knowing that they had all run as well.

As I relayed to the others what I had done, one of them asked if I recalled the rest of what Jesus had told me. I didn't. All I had on my mind that day had been telling Jesus how wrong he was and how I was not going to let him down! So often we miss the bigger picture while focused on our narrow agendas.

"He also said he was praying for you and that when you got back on track, you would be the one to strengthen your brothers and sisters!" they reminded me. Despite my nagging doubts and voice of self-condemnation, I had a glimmer of hope. Maybe God could use me despite my failure.

But I tend to see things as all good or all bad, and it was hard to silence the voice that declared me a failure. I judge myself by my most recent action and see myself as a total success or a total failure based on that. Needless to say, I was not feeling like a success at this point in time. After all, I had denied I knew Jesus. How could I be forgiven for such a thing?

We huddled in an upper room, terrified that the same people that had come for Jesus in the garden would be looking for us.

We bolted the doors down tightly. It felt like all was defeated. It seemed like the journey was over. Then a couple of women came to share that they had been to the tomb and it was empty. They spoke of an angel declaring that Jesus had risen. We wondered if they were delusional, perhaps from a lack of sleep.

Not one to sit there and wonder, I took off with John to check things out for ourselves. Strangely the tomb was empty, just like they told us. But how did we know this meant he was alive? Full of questions, we returned to the upper room. Afraid to hope, and more afraid not to, we sat there caught up in our thoughts. Rumors were flying of other Jesus sightings. But even if he was alive, would he ever want to see me again?

In the midst of our doubts and fears, Jesus appeared. Despite the bars on the door and the barriers of our doubts, Jesus appeared! There he was, telling us not to be afraid and offering us peace.

Encouraged to see him but still struggling with forging myself for what I had done, I regressed into the familiar. I was not sure I was cut out for fishing for men. I would go back to fishing for fish. I was less likely to mess things up that way. Things were easier to control in the fishing business than in the people business. Jesus could find someone else for that.

Several of us were out on the lake when we saw someone on the shore asking how the fishing was going.

"Try casting your nets on the other side," he said.

Within minutes of doing so, we had a familiar experience of a miraculous haul large enough that the nets should have been breaking under the weight.

This was Jesus! Not only had he come looking for me, but he had chosen a place and a memory that was significant to his relationship with me personally.

This was the place where Jesus first called me to fish for people. This is where he had performed the same miracle. This is where he had stepped into my world and invited me into his.

Assured of his forgiveness and reminded of his love, I left the boat full of fish and ran to Jesus.

"Did I love him?" he asked.

Three times, he asked. Three times I assured him, painfully remembering the three times I had denied him. Would I help lead the others? Yes. As much as this hurt, I realized that Jesus was allowing me the chance to make amends and offering me another chance to fish for people. This time I was going to do things his way. This time I was not going to claim more strength than I possessed.

As much as I dislike waiting, I knew I needed to do things his way this time and not mine. We were to wait forty days after he returned to the Father. Then he would send help. He wanted us to spread the word about why he had to suffer and of how he rose again.

Everything in me wanted to get started. Everything in me wanted to go out in my strength, and yet I was growing and learning to wait. I was learning to think before I act. I was learning to accept help. I now knew that I was powerless to change myself, let alone the world.

Upon surrendering my life and will to his care, he sent the Holy Spirit and allowed this broken but humbled man to help change the world. When God tamed my impulsive nature, he gave me boldness to speak without fearing the results. He taught me to accept the things I could not change and the people I could not control. He gave me courage to change the things I could. He helped me to take this sinful world as it is and not as I would have it. He helped me to forgive those who would persecute me for this faith.

And yes, he helped me to not only accept his forgiveness but to forgive myself as well.

Thank you for allowing me to share.

Questions for Reflection:

1. What do you think that was like for Peter and his brother when they left their business to follow Jesus? Have you had anything you believed in enough to take that kind of risk?
2. Can you relate to Peter's tendency to speak now and think later?
3. When have you felt that you were "walking on water" only to lower your eyesight and begin sinking?
4. How do you think Peter felt when he realized he had just denied his Savior? Have you ever had a similar experience or regret?
5. Why do you think Peter went back to fishing?
6. What do you think gave Peter the ability to forgive himself and move forward after what he did? Share how have moved beyond regrets in the past or how you hope to now.
7. Discuss how Peter's understanding shifted from not believing Jesus should suffer to choosing to participate in his sufferings. What helped his accept hardship?

Principles for Recovery:

1. Impulsive decisions can leave irreversible damage.
2. Place your identity in your new name, not your old behaviors.
3. Recognize your limitations and you will limit your relapses.
4. After failure, repent, reflect, regroup, and refocus.
5. Failure is not final; fear is not fatal.

Serving with Serenity

(Martha's Story)

I grew up in a small town called Bethany. My sister, brother, and I were very close. As adults, we lived together and looked out for one another. As the oldest, I tended to take charge and was generally happy to do so. My sister saw me as controlling. Now I know that she was right. I am a grateful follower of Jesus Christ who struggles with codependency, anxiety, and control issues. My name is Martha.

When Mom and Dad died while we were still young, I stepped up to care for my brother, Lazarus, and sister, Mary. It was not easy losing our parents, and I felt responsible for everything around the house. I also saw it as a way to honor my mom's memory. She was always on top of things and worked hard. Now, I did the cooking, cleaning, and countless other household chores. I generally did not complain. I simply did what had to be done. Someone had to do it.

We were blessed to have a relatively large house for our community. We were close enough to Jerusalem (only a couple of miles away) that we often had guests stay in our home. Sometimes they were guests we knew. Our family had lived in the community a long time. Many knew our parents and kept in touch with us after our loss. Others were strangers who were passing through the area and needed lodging. Word got out that our house was available. We always opened our doors for them.

Mary loved to talk with visitors, wanting to find out where they had been and what they had seen in their travels. I served, and I served well. I wanted them to enjoy their stay, and I did all I could to take care of them.

I generally enjoyed serving. I had an eye for details and knew exactly how everything needed to be laid out for dinner. I preferred to know how many would be here and how long they would be staying. I wanted to know what to expect.

After losing both parents, I did everything I could to keep life predictable and avoid surprises. That wasn't always easy.

Mary was a little more laid back in her approach to life. I generally appreciated the fact that she did not interfere with how I wanted to decorate or what I wanted to cook. There were times, however, when it got under my skin to see her sitting, visiting, while I slaved over the fire, cooking dinner for all of the guests she had helped invite. I didn't say anything. I just kept serving. Someone had to do it.

As people came through, we were hearing some interesting accounts about a traveling rabbi named Jesus from Nazareth. It was rumored that he had healed a man who was blind and helped a lame man walk again. Some spoke of other miracles as well. Mary asked all the guests if they had run into Jesus, and if so, what they thought of him.

I listened in from the kitchen and longed for a chance to meet him for myself.

One day we heard that Jesus was going to be in town. We followed the crowd to see where he was teaching. His words grabbed our attention. I heard him say he came to serve and not to be served. *Finally, someone who gets it*, I thought. I also overheard him telling a man who wanted to follow him that he had nowhere to lay his head. *That wasn't right*, I told myself, and went up to him when he was done teaching and invited him to come stay with us for as long as he was in town.

"I have a few of my guys traveling with me. Is that OK?" he asked. "Sure, you are all welcome," I replied. "My brother, Lazarus, went fishing and caught enough fish for all of us!"

We loved having Jesus. Soon he was stopping by every time he was headed to Jerusalem. He had so much wisdom and so many amazing stories.

One day, as was often the case, Mary was sitting listening to his stories and gleaning his wisdom while I was busy preparing something to eat. I just wanted things to be perfect. I had washed everyone's feet. I had double checked the sleeping quarters to be sure everything was in order. I had checked on the desserts in the brick oven. I had fetched some more water from the well. I wanted to be sure that everything was right. Someone had to do it.

My many requests for help had apparently fallen on deaf ears. It was as if Mary did not notice that I was continuing to run around like one of our chickens who had its head cut off, while she just sat and enjoyed the time with Jesus.

Lazarus wasn't much better. I didn't expect as much from him though. He was a man. At least he went out and caught some fish or slaughtered a lamb for dinner some days.

Today, watching Mary became more than I could handle. Then I got an idea. Maybe Jesus could help. After all, he had been around enough that he could see who was doing all the work around here! And he had said he came to serve. He would understand.

"Jesus, doesn't it seem unfair to you that my sister just sits here while I do all the work?"

Surely he would be on my side and would respond with a firm rebuke of her passivity in light of my hard work and hospitality. After all, I was the one who had invited him to dinner in the first place. With confidence that he would see my point, I then went on to boldly tell him what he needed to do.

"Tell her to come and help me!" I demanded.

I was still in denial, and it never occurred to me that it may not be my place to tell other people what they had to do, especially Jesus, the traveling rabbi who I was coming to believe was possibly the Son of God. I told him, nonetheless. In fact, I was a little perturbed that Jesus had not thought of this on his own. There were a lot of things that people did not pick up on and that I had to tell them to do. Someone had to do it.

As much as I wanted Jesus to set her straight, and as unfair as it seemed that I was doing all the work, again, I hoped Jesus would not be too hard on her. I wanted him to be gentle but firm.

She needed to make some changes.

"Martha, Martha!" I heard Jesus saying.

Surely he had not gotten our names mixed up. Why was he using my name? But wait, he was looking straight at me in his reply. His eyes were so gentle and kind.

"Martha, Martha, you are upset and troubled over many things," he continued.

I tried to digest what I was hearing. I could not disagree with him about this. Yes, there are many things to worry about, I wanted to say. Someone has to do it.

I would not have to worry so much if others helped me carry the load.

Then I realized this was not turning out as an affirmation of my concerns but as a rebuke of my priorities.

"There is only one thing worth being concerned about," he concluded. "Mary has discovered it, and it will not be taken away from her." (Luke 10:41-42)

Wow! This was not turning out the way I had intended. Instead of Jesus doing what I asked (OK, demanded) that he do, and rebuking my sister, I was the one being rebuked.

I have to admit that "rebuked" is a strong word, however, considering the gentle manner in which Jesus did so. The way he said my name made it clear that he cared about the fact that I was stressed, and his eyes removed any doubt that he wanted what was best for me as well. He genuinely cared that I was missing out on something that Mary was gaining.

He was firm, though, in setting a boundary toward my controlling ways. No, he was not going to rebuke Mary, and he was not OK with this choice being taken away from her. She was getting something that he wanted to give both of us, but I was too distracted to receive it.

Interestingly, Jesus never told me to stop serving. He never told me that I was a bad person for my choices. He showed me by example that we are not to force others to change or become like us. We cannot do their inventory, make their amends, or force them to change. We are each responsible for our choices.

Jesus indicated, however, that Mary had chosen well, and I was forced to examine my own priorities. I did not stop serving, but I did stop controlling. And I began listening more to what Jesus had to say, even though it was often from behind the kitchen sink. As I listened, my faith was growing.

As my faith grew, I worried less. I served more from joy and less from feeling that someone had to do it! I chose to serve some days and to slow down and listen on others.

One of the people I loved to serve was my brother. Lazarus and I were close. It hit me hard when I saw him so sick. I waited on him night and day, making him soups and giving him every herb that I thought might help. This wasn't like the other times, however, and he was getting extremely weak.

Soon I began to realize that he was not going to get better. Then it hit me; we could send for Jesus! He loved Lazarus. He loved all of us. I had seen him heal every disease imaginable. He would come and he would heal him—I was sure of it! I sent a runner to find him immediately.

My spirits lifted, but not for long.

As I watched Lazarus struggling to breathe, I could not understand why Jesus had not come. As I held my brother's hand when he mouthed one last "I love you," I wondered why Jesus hadn't even sent word. I knew he cared, but at this moment my heart was flooded with a combination of grief, hurt, and anger.

Where was he when we needed him most? Lazarus was gone. Was he ever going to come? Was it because of the dangers last time he was in the area and people tried to stone him? Was that why he hadn't come?

It was four days from the time of Lazarus's death, and we were getting ready for the funeral when I heard that Jesus had been spotted on the other side of town. As much as I was hurting, I needed to see Jesus and be with him in this time of grief. Mary waited with the other guests.

The old Martha would have felt obligated to stay at the house and keep serving, to stay busy, to keep things under control. I was learning priorities, however, and I knew that I needed a few minutes with Jesus alone before all the others surrounded him. I was learning to be assertive in taking care of myself and not just everyone else.

"Lord, if only you had been here, my brother would not have died," I lamented and poured my heart out to him. Then, without knowing for sure whether to even ask, I went on, "But even now, I know that God will give you whatever you ask." (John 11:21-22)

The old Martha would have told Jesus what to do and how to do it. I had told everyone what to do. Now I humbly threw out a thought that maybe there was still hope of some kind, even as I knew it was up to Jesus what he chose to do. I was surrendering my will to his control and no longer making demands.

As I watched Jesus interact with Mary, me, and others in our grief, I was struck by his compassion as well as his genuine love and care for all that we felt. As he stood there weeping, I was not sure if he was weeping for his own loss or out of his great love for us. I had seen Jesus in a lot of settings, but never in this context.

As he saw the pain and agony that this loss rendered upon those he loved, it appeared that Jesus was angry. Perhaps it all hit him, in experiencing with humanity the very reason he was about to go to the cross and the curse of death that we all faced. Whatever the reasons, I know that Jesus felt many of the

RECOVERING FROM DYSFUNCTION • 155

emotions we all felt in times of loss, including anger. I felt closer to him than ever knowing that he shared in our grief and in our humanity.

My faith was still a work in progress. When Jesus spoke of my brother rising again, I assumed he meant in the great resurrection to come. I had come to believe that Jesus was the Messiah indeed, the very Son of God. This I knew for certain.

When and how my brother would rise, I was not so sure. Even when we got to the tomb, I hesitated when he said to have the stone rolled away. It didn't cross my mind that he could control the odor from the body, let alone that he was about to restore that body right in front of my eyes.

Next thing I knew, Jesus was praying, thanking God the Father for hearing him. The Son of God, who had just demonstrated his role as the Son of Man, then made it clear that he did indeed have the power over death. "Lazarus, come out!" he shouted.

With a mixture of laughter over the humor in seeing a man wrapped in grave clothes hobbling out, trying to break free, and a reverential awe of what had just taken place, we stood there staring in disbelief!

Nobody said a word.

Finally, Jesus broke our silence, "Unwrap him and let him go!" he said.

You would think that no one would have to tell us that, but he did. Our tears had turned to shock, and now our shock turned to an exhilarating celebration. Mary was the first to embrace Lazarus. When I got to him, I held him so tight, he had to ask me to let go.

The hardest thing about trials and about learning to trust is that you don't understand the reasons until later. I knew Jesus had boundaries, and I had to believe that he had a good reason for not coming to heal my brother.

I had to accept the things I could not change and trust his will over mine. I had to choose to believe even when I did not understand. Now, standing there with Lazarus, Mary, and Jesus, I cried with tears of joy and relief.

My faith turned to sight when I saw how many people came to faith in Jesus out of the miracle of my brother's resurrection. You should have seen the look on the face of that one man who walked fifteen miles to pay his respects to a Lazarus he thought had died.

"Are you looking for my grave?" Lazarus asked jovially when we saw the man down in the cemetery.

Losing Lazarus and now having him back helped change all of us. Lazarus had a new love for Jesus and a willingness to tell anyone who would listen what Jesus had done for him. Mary clung all the more to every word that Jesus spoke and every lesson that he taught. I chose to spend more time sitting with my brother and sister and appreciated the time that we had together. Instead of trying to control and fix things, I was becoming better at accepting them.

One of the things I was learning to accept was the difference in personality between Mary and myself. She not only loved to sit and listen to others, but she was a deep thinker. Whereas I had the gift of serving, she had the gift of giving. Neither was wrong as long as we did what we did out of love and not codependency or obligation.

Mary's gift of giving was evident one of those last visits Jesus paid us before he went to the cross. While everyone sat talking and listening to Jesus, Mary took an expensive bottle of perfume, one of the few memories from Mom's collection, and poured it out on Jesus's feet, wiping his feet with her own hair.

In the past, I would have been upset. Once again I was serving while she was sitting. This time, however, I was serving joyfully and not with resentment. I was choosing to serve while respecting Mary's choice to sit. I also appreciated the fact that she was exercising her gift to love Jesus just like I was. Others, particularly one disciple who handled the money, looked on Mary with judgment and called her sacrifice wasteful. I looked on her with pride. This was my little sister. She understood what was about to happen, and she had chosen to literally pour out her love on Jesus.

While a lot of the disciples were heartbroken over Jesus's death upon the cross, my siblings and I were hopeful. We had heard him speak of his impending crucifixion, like the others had, but we also had heard him mention a resurrection on the third day. Thanks to Mary, we had all learned to listen a little bit more and thanks to Lazarus, we had learned to hope. Death was not the final word for Jesus Christ of Nazareth!

It was no surprise for us when we started hearing the rumors that Jesus was alive! We knew what he came to do, and we knew that he was the Son of God and that his sacrifice for our sins would be accepted. While others clamored to be the first to find him, we had learned a few things that helped us wait until he showed up for dinner.

Jesus had boundaries, and he followed a timetable, one that we did not have to control. Jesus would be here when it was the right time for Jesus to be here. We respected his timing. When he did show up, we were ready. Lazarus slaughtered a lamb, Mary washed his feet, and I served dinner (yes, someone still had to do it), but we all sat and soaked in his every word.

This was my Messiah, the one who died for my sins. This was the one who had taught me to let go of my need for perfection and control, to serve out of choice and not codependency, and to set priorities that put people over things and love over control.

Perhaps someone hearing my story today has also gone through something traumatic, and perhaps you also try to compensate with control and predictability. Perhaps you utilize worry and the pursuit of perfection to make sure something bad never happens to you or your family again.

I know what that is like. I also know what it is like to be free. It will not come overnight, but freedom is possible, and faith is the key. I hope that you will release those things that you cannot control into the hands of the one who can control all things. And I hope that God uses my story to help you learn to respect the choices of those around you who may have different gifts than you but have the same heart and the same Lord.

Thanks for letting me share.

Questions for Reflection:

1. How was Martha expecting Jesus to respond to her? Why?
2. Have you dealt with difficult losses or unpredictability in your life? If so, how have you tried to cope with that?
3. What changes do you see between the old Martha and the new one?
4. When is serving the right thing, and how does it become a wrong thing?
5. When have you had to hold onto faith despite the feeling that God should have done things differently or showed up sooner?
6. The author suggests Martha's heart toward Mary likely changed. How does it help your relationships when you learn to let go? How about when you don't?

Principles for Recovery:

1. Your roles as a child impact your reactions as an adult.
2. The service of your hands is less important than the state of your heart.
3. The more you "need" to control your surroundings, the less you are able to control your emotions.
4. When you stop to listen, God will give you strength to live.

From Rejection to Redemption

(Zacchaeus's Story)

I was not the most popular guy to invite to a party. Actually, people tended to avoid me everywhere I went. They walked on the other side of the street and cowered in fear when I crossed over to their side. It was not always this way. But now I was a chief tax collector who had the ability to levy fees and collect fines as I saw fit. I was materialistic, a thief, and a liar. My name is Zacchaeus.

Because I was short, I was often the object of jokes.

"Stand up, Zacchaeus!" they would yell in a crowd. "Oh, you are standing up. Sorry about that."

I stayed home a lot to avoid the laughter and bullying on the streets of Jericho. Home was my safe haven.

"Don't let them get to you," my mom would say. "They may be bigger than you, but you are smarter than all of them. You will show them one day."

Her encouragement helped me believe that I was capable of something other than joining a circus or playing the role of a midget in the school play, like my classmates suggested.

The day a bully took all my shekels and gave me two black eyes, I determined I was not going to be on the receiving end of this anymore.

I struggled to my feet, aching as I walked home. I saw a man who looked not much bigger than me and certainly not stronger. He seemed in control, giving orders to one of his henchmen. The man was beating a much larger man to a pulp, crying out, "This is what happens when you don't pay what you owe me!"

I had seen this man before and asked around to see what he did and how he came to command such fear and respect on the streets. I was told that he was a tax collector. Apparently it was his job to collect taxes for the Romans, and if people refused, he was given the authority to enforce this by inflicting whatever physical punishment he deemed necessary to teach them a lesson and ensure compliance in the future.

"You want to do what?" my parents reacted as I told them of what I wanted to be when I grew up.

"Nobody likes a tax collector. They work for the Romans and are considered traitors," my dad explained.

"Well," I replied, "nobody likes me anyway, and at least people would respect me."

Despite their objections, I remained steadfast. I was going to be a tax collector. I was going to be the guy that others feared one day. Every beating after this, I recalled what I had seen and reminded myself that one day I was going to be the one with the power and control, not the other way around.

Power was one motivator. The other was money. I was drawn to the financial perks that I witnessed the more that I studied the tax collectors and their profession. I told myself that I was not going to put my family through the same financial stress that I grew up under. My children would have the best sandals and not the ones with holes in the bottom like I had to wear every day.

Chances are that with my DNA, they would also be short and have enough jokes about their stature. I did not want them exposed to any other unnecessary jokes and laughter. I can't say that my only motivator was my children, but that made it seem less selfish than to admit that I wanted more stuff for myself as well.

I started as an apprentice. It was strange how the guy who trained me seemed to lack the fulfilment and enjoyment of the power that I expected him to enjoy. I overlooked this, however, and assumed that he had lost an appreciation for what he had.

After all, he could tell people how much they owed, when they owed it, and how they had to pay it. He had the Roman government behind him to enforce whatever he needed to enforce. He made enough to pay off those he wanted to and to entice all the young ladies who were drawn to his money and position on the streets.

People feared him the same way I was determined to be feared one day. Sure, people talked about him behind his back, but I never saw anyone disrespect him to his face—not if they knew what was good for them.

I watched how he set up and how he tracked people down. I saw his little tricks where he would put down a number on his ledger and pocket the difference from what he had told the person before him. I wondered if the Romans would come after him for this, but it was apparent that as long as they got what they expected, they couldn't care less what else he charged or how he collected.

It wasn't long before I was given my own section of town. Soon I was taxing for land, for food, for animals, for walking down the street! The bullies who had grown up and now worked the fields or cared for livestock soon learned who was in control. It felt good, at least for a while, to see fear and dread in the eyes of those who I used to fear myself.

The money was good. I felt guilty initially when I charged more than I was supposed to and lied to people in the community. Soon, however, I was well versed in the rationalizations and excuses that I made for doing so.

After all, if I didn't do it, someone else would be doing the same thing or worse. I deserved better than what I had been given in my life, and now I was getting what was owed me. Surely I was justified in what I was doing, especially since every other tax collector was doing the exact same thing.

While the money opened doors for entertainment and self-gratifying pleasures, it did not help me secure lasting relationships or the deeper friendships that I longed for. Being able to control and intimidate others helped keep them in line but never helped establish trust.

Without trust and freedom, love can never flourish. Without loving relationships, I soon learned that it is a lonely and empty existence.

The emptiness was compounded by a lack of connection with God. As Solomon said in his own search, "Everything is meaningless . . . completely meaningless!" (Ecclesiastes 1:2)

Until we find something outside ourselves, something that can give meaning to our lives, we simply try to fill the void. We end up always longing for more and never feeling fulfilled.

Around the time that I began to perceive my own spiritual bankruptcy and relational isolation, I began to hear people on the street talking about a teacher named Jesus Christ from Nazareth. I heard a lot on the streets. I did not always know what was true and what was not.

After hearing the same story over and over, however, about healings and gestures of kindness, I wanted to see for myself what this was all about. They said Jesus was heading toward our part of town within the next few hours.

Being short, I naturally always hated crowds. Unless I could work my way to the front, my view typically consisted of a man's robe, a woman's long hair flowing down her back, or the top of a child's head. It was useless to go anywhere if I wanted to see whoever or whatever we were all clamoring to see. I usually stayed home.

Then there was the disdain. Despite my ability to command fear from others when I was in charge of collecting a tax or levying a fine, I knew where I stood with others in town, and I could see the contempt in their eyes.

I knew that people were unlikely to help me get to the front of the line, but I was determined!

A neighbor had heard Jesus teach and shared a quote with me. He said he had come for the spiritually and emotionally sick, to bring healing to people who needed it—not those who had their lives all in order. I couldn't get that idea out of my head. If this was true, I wanted to know. I wanted to see if indeed Jesus had more to say about coming to help someone as spiritually empty as myself. It was worth doing whatever it took to find the answer.

It had been a long time since I had climbed a tree. I was pretty good at it when I was a child. The idea hit me when I saw people lining the streets and jockeying for position on the projected path of Jesus's journey into town.

I looked ahead to see if it could be done. Sure enough, ahead of the crowd and somewhat out of sight there was a sycamore tree with a limb within reach. Perhaps if I got up there before others noticed, I could hide in some of the branches near the top and avoid detection.

Nobody seemed to notice me climb, and everyone's attention was focused on someone else and not Zacchaeus on this day. As I waited, swatting mosquitos and keeping in the shaded branches, I heard people shouting.

"I can see! I can see! Jesus healed me and now I can see!" one man shouted for joy as he ran ahead of the crowd. He was running like a child and obviously trying to take in every sight that he had never been able to witness.

I remained undetected as the crowd surrounding Jesus came closer. I found myself getting nervous but also anticipating what it was that I would hear Jesus say to the others, as he was now almost directly in front of my hiding place. Was he really as kind as others had said, or would he be blasting the sinners and the traitors, the liars and the tax collectors, as many other religious prophets were known to do?

Either way, I would remain still and listen closely in this place of safety.

Sometimes you are not as hidden as you think you are. Many times, people see more than you realize they do—more of your brokenness, your emptiness, and your lies and deception.

I heard him say something about wanting "all those who are weary, burdened, and tired" (Matthew 11:28) to come to him so that he could give them rest.

What a promise! I was utterly captivated watching his every move and listening to his every word. He stopped right under the very tree branch I was hiding in. He looked up right into my eyes, with a smile. That smile acknowledged my desire to be anonymous but also cared about my desire to be in relationship.

"Come down, Zacchaeus. I am going over to your house today," Jesus said.

I felt like I must be dreaming. How did this stranger know my name? Had he heard about me? If he had, it could not have been good! But he wasn't looking at me with eyes that glared with condemnation but rather with eyes that glistened with compassion.

He looked as though he knew my heart's every desire and accepted me despite my every failure.

I had a huge house. Business was good. I was not only a tax collector but had been promoted to regional director. I knew all the tricks for collecting. Despite all that I cheated and lied about and collected for myself, I always made sure that I gave enough to the government of Rome so they knew they could count on me.

I had other tax collectors and government officials over for lavish feasts, but the average person in my community had never been inside the doors of my house, except for those who I employed to clean, serve, or decorate. I was not used to having a band of travelers stopping by. Despite the custom of our day, to entertain travelers and invite strangers in was not something I generally practiced.

I was not the generous type.

What a surprise. Jesus saw me when nobody else did.

It was as if he was looking for me. It was as if he knew where I was. I wondered, as a million thoughts ran through my head, if he really was looking for the emotionally and spiritually sick and tired. If so, he had nailed it.

Not only did he see me, but he invited himself to my house. It was as if he knew I would not have the confidence to invite him over. I did not even expect him to see me or speak to me, let alone stay overnight at my house! Now, here we were, on our way to my house. Me and Jesus—this amazing miracle-working teacher from Nazareth.

You would think that this would be intimidating, and in some ways. it was. I knew I did not stand for the same values as a religious leader like Jesus. I knew I had taken things that did not belong to me and charged things that were not fair. I knew that my methods of enforcing control were far different than this meek and kindhearted rabbi from Nazareth.

Yet I felt loved and accepted by someone I had just met, in a way that I never had in my entire life.

While the others were settling down and waiting on dinner, I saw a familiar face among the followers of Jesus.

"Is that really you, Levi?" I asked, startled to see one of my fellow tax collectors from years gone by.

Though we worked in different areas, we tax collectors stuck together. Being isolated and rejected from those that saw us as traitors and crooks, it gave some comfort to get together. I sure did not expect to see a fellow tax collector as part of Jesus's disciples.

I had wondered what happened to him and why he was not at the last couple of tax collector conventions.

"It's me. Most people call me Matthew now," he replied with a laugh.

"Matthew?" I teased. "You must have made some changes."

I knew the name Matthew means "true." He had made some changes indeed. Maybe it was true and Jesus did welcome all of us, including me.

As I listened to Jesus speak and watched him interact with all of us, I didn't need any convincing. This man truly was the Messiah. He was the only power that could help bring sanity back into my life. He really cared about the broken and the destitute.

The irony was that some of the poor people whom he championed and reached out to were those same people that had become that way through the abuse of power from people like me. Yes, he was their advocate and also mine. How easily he seemed to go back and forth from talking to the poor and the affluent, the Jews, the Romans, the educated, and the illiterate. His band of followers were an eclectic bunch.

One thing was becoming very clear to me. I was ready to embrace this Jesus. I was ready to leave behind a life of selfishness and greed. I was tired of my way, of the world's way. I was ready to surrender my life and will to his control.

I was not sure what this was going to look like. All I knew was that I was ready to make some changes. Jesus did not point his fingers at me and verbalize every wrong behavior or motive that he saw in me. He didn't have to.

Being in his presence was enough to show me what it means to love unconditionally and live unconventionally. Being part of his community, as brief as it had been, convinced me that there was a way out of emptiness and a way into wholeness. I knew in my heart what had to change. I determined to take the next step.

"Jesus," I declared, not caring who heard or what they thought, "I am ready to give half of what I own to those less fortunate."

That, in itself, sounded noble and admitted no guilt. It was the next part that was hardest to say, knowing the implications that came with it.

"If I have cheated anyone, I will repay them up to four times what I took," I added, choking back tears.

There was no doubt I had cheated many individuals, and perhaps I was still working my way out of denial to use the word "if." *Who was I kidding? There were plenty of witnesses in the room who knew firsthand that I had cheated someone.* Levi (or Matthew, I should say) gave me a knowing look and smiled. *Yes, I would definitely be paying some people back.* There was no "if" about it!

Maybe Matthew could serve as my sponsor and help make sure I stayed out of denial. I definitely would need someone to keep me honest on this journey, and I would need encouragement in this process of making amends. There was going to be a lot of it.

Upon hearing my confession and seeing my change of heart, Jesus got everyone's attention and wanted to let them know that what they were seeing was an example of the kind of change that happens when we come to him in faith and surrender our lives to him. While I was barely getting started on this journey, I saw already that each of our stories is a significant part of his story and that Jesus was not going to waste any of our mistakes. He was already taking mine and teaching others from it.

The last thing Jesus said was, "The Son of Man came to seek and to save those who are lost." (Luke 19:10) Yes, I was lost. I was lost in my pursuit of material gain, at the cost of my spiritual integrity. I was lost in my need to control, at the cost of the respect from my community. I was so lost in my bitterness as a victim that I did not care who I victimized in the pursuit of power. By pursuing power, I had lost control. Now, by releasing control, I was gaining freedom.

Jesus had come to seek a tax collector who others had come to despise and reject. By accepting me as I was, he gave me the freedom to see who I could become. By accepting my powerless state, I came to experience his power to change that state.

If you are feeling lost spiritually, please know that there is a power greater than you who is pursuing you. His name is Jesus. He is looking for you even while you are hiding in the branches of shame. He wants to spend time with you even if you have shut yourself off from him and others. He knows your name, just like he did mine, and he wants to come over to your house. I hope you will allow him to do so. I am sure glad I did. Thank you for letting me share my story.

Questions for Reflection:

1. Have you ever felt rejected or unpopular? If so, did any of this relate to your choices or further influence your choices? How?
2. Why do you think Jesus made it a point to stay with Zacchaeus?
3. How do you imagine the disciples reacted when they realized where their leader was taking them for dinner? How would you have reacted?
4. What were the changes that Zacchaeus made? What made this possible?
5. How do you feel about the idea of Jesus looking for you? Are you ready to make any changes? If so, share what those are.

Principles for Recovery:

1. No matter how far you fall, God will be waiting where you land.
2. When you are ready for recovery, you will do what it takes for recovery.
3. Inventory without amends leaves regrets without recovery.
4. A sponsor who has been there will help you not go back there.

Conclusion

What's your story?

Hopefully you have connected with some of the stories in this book. Maybe you even saw yourself in some of its pages. If nothing else, I hope that you recognized the glaring truth that God never gives up on us even when we may give up on ourselves. God is the great redeemer. He takes our brokenness and rebuilds and reshapes us for a larger purpose. His family is big enough to include you, and his love is deep enough to embrace any dysfunction you may bring with you.

Where are you in your journey? Perhaps you are already in recovery and have told your story as well. If so, you know the freedom that comes in sharing and letting go of the secrets that can keep us stuck. Or maybe you are still at the beginning. Perhaps you are wondering if there is hope, or how in the world God can take the mess you have found yourself in and turn it into a purpose. Maybe you are seeing some hope that God does indeed recycle the pain of our past, to produce a purpose for our future. Yes, you can be a masterpiece of his grace.

My prayer is that you will not limit yourself or the power of God. Where you have been does not have to determine where you are going. It didn't for the people in these pages. God is bigger than your past and bigger than your failures. He has dreams for you. He will not waste what you have been through. He is the great recycler!

If you are looking for others who have found this same hope and who can walk this journey with you, reach out to a recovery group such as Celebrate Recovery near you. There is hope and support, and you do not have to take this journey alone!

Printed in the United States
By Bookmasters